THE CLINIC

Tristaine Book One

What Reviewers Say About Bold Strokes Authors

KIM BALDWIN

"'A riveting novel of suspense' seems to be a very overworked phrase. However, it is extremely apt when discussing Kim Baldwin's [*Hunter's Pursuit*]. An exciting page turner [features] Katarzyna Demetrious, a bounty hunter...with a million dollar price on her head. Look for this excellent novel of suspense..." – **R. Lynne Watson**, *MegaScene*

RONICA BLACK

"Black juggles the assorted elements of her first book, [*In Too Deep*], with assured pacing and estimable panache...[including]...the relative depth—for genre fiction—of the central characters: Erin, the married-but-separated detective who comes to her lesbian senses; loner Patricia, the policewoman-mentor who finds herself falling for Erin; and sultry club owner Elizabeth, the sexually predatory suspect who discards women like Kleenex...until she meets Erin."– **Richard Labonte**, *Book Marks, Q Syndicate, 2005*

ROSE BEECHAM

"...her characters seem fully capable of walking away from the particulars of whodunit and engaging the reader in other aspects of their lives." – *Lambda Book Report*

GUN BROOKE

"*Course of Action* is a romance...populated with a host of captivating and amiable characters. The glimpses into the lifestyles of the rich and beautiful people are rather like guilty pleasures....[A] most satisfying and entertaining reading experience." – **Arlene Germain**, reviewer for the *Lambda Book Report* and the *Midwest Book Review*

JANE FLETCHER

"*The Walls of Westernfort* is not only a highly engaging and fast-paced adventure novel, it provides the reader with an interesting framework for examining the same questions of loyalty, faith, family and love that [the characters] must face." – **M. J. Lowe**, *Midwest Book Review*

RADCLY*f*FE

"...well-honed storytelling skills...solid prose and sure-handedness of the narrative..." – **Elizabeth Flynn**, *Lambda Book Report*

"...well-plotted...lovely romance...I couldn't turn the pages fast enough!" – **Ann Bannon**, author of *The Beebo Brinker Chronicles*

Visit us at www.boldstrokesbooks.com

THE CLINIC

TRISTAINE BOOK ONE

by

Cate Culpepper

2006

THE CLINIC

ISBN 1-933110-42-2
THIS TRADE PAPERBACK IS PUBLISHED BY
BOLD STROKES BOOKS, INC.,
NEW YORK, USA

FIRST EDITION: JUSTICE HOUSE PUBLISHING 2001
SECOND EDITION: BOLD STROKES BOOKS, INC., MAY 2006

CREDITS

EDITORS: CINDY CRESAP AND SHELLEY THRASHER
PRODUCTION DESIGN: J. BARRE GREYSTONE
COVER ART: TOBIAS BRENNER (http://www.tobiasbrenner.de/)
COVER GRAPHIC: SHERI (graphicartist2020@hotmail.com)

Acknowledgments

I'm very grateful for the support of Radclyffe and the fine women of Bold Strokes Books. The second edition of *The Clinic* is a better novel thanks to my editor, Cindy Cresap. Jay Csokmay provided great feedback and encouragement. Warm thanks to Jenny, Eva, Dana, and all the Amazons on the Tristaine mailing list for their infinite patience and moral support.

DEDICATION

To the women of Shann's Clan:
Jay, Monica, Dana and Lisa
We will go home someday

CHAPTER ONE

The steel doors at the end of the cell block parted with a resounding crash.

"They're not taking you, Jesstin."

"Stand down, Cam." Jess rested her hand on the younger woman's shoulder. "It might be another interrogation."

"They bring you back bloody from those," Kyla hissed. Her brown eyes flashed both anger and fear as heavy footfalls moved down the stone hallway. "And what if it isn't, Jess? What if they're here to—?"

"Then tell Shann I died Tristaine's true daughter." Jess eyed them both. "We can't fight bullets and truncheons with our fists, adanin. Save your strength for the real battle."

"All right, Amazon." The lead guard waited until the five other armed staff gathered close to the small cell. "Stand away from the door."

"We're all Amazons, you dim City prick," Kyla spat.

"Watch your mouth, little whore." The guard nodded down the hall, and someone threw a switch to open the barred gate.

It was still moving when Camryn flew at the men with the deadly ferocity of a warrior twice her age. Jess cursed and dove after her, and Kyla was only a heartbeat slower. The next moments were filled with roars of alarm and the thudding of clubs on flesh. It finally took a shower of mace to restrain Jess and force the younger Amazons back into the cell.

"I wouldn't pull that shit where you're going, banshee." The red-faced commander jutted his chin toward Jess's sisters, who lay gasping and raging on the concrete floor. "Not if you want to see those two alive again."

The beating that followed seemed senseless. The guards didn't fire questions at Jess, as they had in the past. They simply battered her until she couldn't stand. She swayed on her knees, bleeding from a cut over one eye, until a cudgel smashed into the side of her head and took her down. As her senses faded she heard Kyla's voice calling her, choked and despairing.

As long as they leave Kyla and Camryn alone, Jess thought. *As long as they're okay, we can give Shann time.*

She was unconscious when she was transferred to the Clinic.

❖

Biting cold woke her.

Jess surfaced through the familiar, unpleasant haze bestowed by blows to the head. She found herself strapped into a jointed chair, a kind of recliner, equipped with arm and ankle cuffs. Her long body lay full length on its padded surface, and the cuffs were tight but not biting. She figured if she hadn't been freezing and aching with fresh bruises, she'd be comfortable enough.

Another intense light flooded over her, courtesy of an arc lamp suspended over the recliner. It took Jess several tries to squint her eyes fully open. She still wore Prison blacks, a standard-issue sleeveless shirt and slacks, and she was barefoot. Her wrists were cuffed to the chair at her sides. Her ankles were similarly bound to the base of the recliner.

She shifted, wincing at the pain in her side, her gaze ticking methodically around the small, antiseptic room. A detention cell, judging by the heavy steel door, empty except for the reclining restraint and shelves of medical supplies, and cold as a Fed's heart. The frigid air smelled astringently sterile. With a nostalgia that was almost grief, Jess longed for the light pine spice of Tristaine's mountain breezes. She wondered if this eye-watering chemical stench would burn it from her memory forever.

Jess knew where she was. Horror stories of this place abounded in the Prison population. Tales of the research done here had even reached Tristaine. If half the rumors about the Clinic were true, Jess might have opted for execution over transfer, given a choice.

She shivered and craned her neck. She couldn't see the cooling unit in the wall behind her, but judging from the chill blasting through the cell, it was cranked high. She lay still and concentrated on her breathing. The crease between her arched eyebrows faded as she relaxed. Jess knew she wasn't badly hurt. She was cold and hungry, but she'd been hungry for weeks. She still had a pulse. She could wait this part out.

Camryn and Kyla were relatively safe, the young idiots. They'd been arrested in a brazen attempt to free Jess, mistaking their adolescent selves for the seasoned warriors celebrated around Tristaine's storyfires. If Shann hadn't been sick with her own grief for Dyan, she would have realized Cam and Ky couldn't abide the thought of Jess rotting in a City Prison. The women of Tristaine were adanin, sisters, and they watched out for each other.

Jess wondered how long her respite would last before someone came for her and this bleak nightmare continued. She was too cold to sleep, so she allowed herself the rare luxury of remembering home. To her lifelong dismay, she had no control over her tear ducts. She hated it, but she cried easily and always had. Her mentor, Dyan, taught her warriors never to shed tears before an enemy. Jess didn't risk remembering Tristaine now unless she was alone.

Her shoulders relaxed against the leather surface of the restrainer, and her breathing deepened as her mind filled with images. Nothing drawn out, just quick flickering images of her sisters and her village.

All the clichés of poetry applied to Tristaine: sunlit meadows and craggy, brooding peaks, surrounded by the lush thickness of old-growth forest. The mountain air was as crisp and pure as chilled wine and vibrant with birdsong. A river coursed through the center of the village, wending between their cabins and lodges. Its quiet, rushing music nurtured the daughters of Tristaine, even in their sleep. Through the long, bleak City nights, Jess still ached for that reassuring whisper.

She summoned faces, and they came. Shann and Dyan, sitting quietly in meetings of Tristaine's high council, listening more than speaking, their hands joined loosely on the oak table. Dyan's scarred knuckles, her blunt fingers stroking Shann's wrist. Kyla's sweet, rich soprano, raised in song at a harvest festival dance.

Camryn's younger blood sister, Lauren, following Dyan around everywhere she went like a worshipful puppy. She blushed crimson whenever Dyan spoke to her and raised her hand to hide her crooked front teeth when she smiled.

Jess's eyes filled as more brutal memories surfaced. Riding a routine patrol on a moonlit mountain trail, at Dyan's side. The ambush by City soldiers, and Dyan falling under a deadly spray of bullets. Little Lauren dying seconds later. Jess shivered and shook her head slightly to banish those wrenching images.

She heard the pneumatic pump over the door whoosh as a young blond woman elbowed it open. She was carrying a clipboard, and she wore a white coat. Some kind of healer. Jess blinked rapidly, stinging the cut over her eye.

"What the—?" There was surprise in the girl's voice. The white coat was too big for her, and she wrapped it more tightly around her shoulders as she went to check the cooling unit behind the jointed chair. Jess noted that she moved like an athlete, in spite of her diminutive size.

She studied Jess's restraints silently for a moment, and her green eyes narrowed when she saw the emerging bruises on the prisoner's face. Then she sighed and blinked at the steam her breath made in the cold air.

"My name is Brenna. I'm your medical advocate." She

consulted the form on her clipboard. "Who left you in here like this?"

"Hello, Brenna." Jess flexed her sore jaw. "I'm Jesstin."

Brenna blew tousled bangs off her forehead and slapped the clipboard against her thigh. "Well, this tells me exactly jack. You came in when, last night?" Without waiting for a reply, she snatched the penlight out of the breast pocket of her white coat, thumbed it on, and moved the beam across Jess's glassy eyes. "Were you examined on arrival, Jesstin?"

"No. I'm all right." It would have sounded butch if her teeth hadn't been chattering.

Brenna measured Jess's pulse at the throat and frowned at her bloodshot eyes. "How long since you've had any solid sleep or a decent meal?"

"A while."

Brenna muttered something derogatory about Prison health-care services as she palpated the base of Jess's jaw. Judging from her contusions, both fresh and faded, her patient had been beaten more than once in the recent past. Brenna wondered uneasily what this prisoner, with her mild brogue, had done to merit such abuse.

For her part, Jess wondered when the Feds had started handing out hypodermics to school kids. At least this girl had good instincts. Her touch was light and careful, and her green eyes had that same look of focused concentration that Shann's held when she tended Tristaine's wounded. She doubtless had excellent training. City dwellers were tested for aptitude in childhood, then educated rigorously in a single discipline. Jess hoped this Brenna had held no dreams of teaching or practicing law.

Jess tightened as Brenna's fingers probed a tender area low on her right side, and Brenna instantly shot her a look of concern before continuing. This little pixie didn't seem callous enough for Government work.

"Were you given anything for pain at the Prison?" Brenna asked.

"They don't keep analgesics at the Prison. Your hands are cold, Brenna."

"Jesstin?" Brenna straightened. "You're supposed to answer my questions as simply and briefly as possible. If you're insolent, or too familiar, or uncooperative, there'll be consequences. You know that, right?"

"Right."

"Great, we understand each other." Brenna pulled a thick blanket from the stand beneath the restraining chair. "You may be bigger than me, but in your condition I could deck you with one punch. Don't forget it, please." She flipped the blanket out and settled it over Jess, then tucked it around her sides with that odd gentleness. "Okay. I'll find someone in maintenance to turn down the damn cooler. We'll make you comfortable enough to rest. Sound all right?"

"Yes'm."

Brenna glanced at Jess warily, but her sky blue eyes were guileless. She nodded and left the cell.

❖

Brenna slapped her clipboard on the executive secretary's desk. "Charlotte, I need to see Caster."

Charlotte batted heavy eyelids at her. "Goodness, Brenna. Is there a problem with your patient?"

"Yes. Is Caster in?"

"Well, she is, but generally she's not available on demand, you know." Charlotte smiled sympathetically, and her penciled eyebrows rose. "Military Research is really nothing like the Civilian unit, sweetie. Now you're working with the top scientists in the City, and you can't expect them to be at the beck and call of every entry-level—"

"It's quite all right, Charlotte." An elegant woman with a silver cloud of hair and a patrician carriage emerged from the office behind the desk. "My door is always open to my staff, particularly this brilliant young medic who's so vital to our current study."

"Oh, well, that's fine then." Charlotte flushed. "Brenna, you are so incredibly lucky to be working with Caster. You know she received *another* Government citation only last week? Let me bring you two some coffee. It won't—"

"Thank you, Charlotte, but we can't take you away from your busy desk. Come, Brenna, walk with me." Caster took Brenna's elbow and steered her gently down the richly carpeted corridor. "I hope you're not in need of a caffeine fix, dear. I can take only so much fawning before noon. Now tell me, how are you finding your first days with us?"

"I have some concerns, Caster." Brenna drew a breath. She wasn't easily intimidated, but the scientist's regal aura demanded deference. "Our test subject was transferred from the Prison last night, and not only was she badly beaten before arrival, no one—"

"Ah, our Tristainian is here at last." Caster beamed. "Do you know what lengths we had to go to in order to secure a subject for this study, Brenna? Why, it took months of planning and coordination with a dozen different Federal agencies." She paused, and the fingers on Brenna's arm tightened. "Jesstin is fully functional, isn't she? No bones were broken, no organs ruptured?"

"I haven't done a full physical, but there was nothing critical on initial exam. However, whoever did the transfer just dumped her in a detention cell, Caster, and she lay in restraints for hours without medical attention. And some idiot cranked up the cooler in there so high she—"

"All quite deliberate, Brenna." Caster smiled at her stunned expression. "For this study, our subject must be kept in a state of constant vulnerability. For some prisoners, psychological duress is enough. But Jesstin, as you've probably noticed, is quite a formidable physical specimen, and she doesn't frighten easily.

It's vital that she understand we have complete and utter mastery over her fate, and unfortunately, the only way to remind her of that is through punitive dominance."

"Punitive dominance," Brenna repeated. She pulled her white coat closely around her and folded her arms. "I…I see, Caster. I'm sorry, it's just a very…different way of handling things than the protocols I'm used to."

"I'm sure it is, dear." Caster slipped an arm around her shoulders. "You came to us from the Civilian unit, and their clinical approach differs greatly from ours. On the C.U., you worked primarily with petty criminals, artists, religious zealots, and the like, testing new medications. Here, your patients will be felons. Murderers, political dissidents, arsonists. Prisoners who present a genuine, ongoing threat to Government security."

"All right, Caster." Brenna hated the meekness in her voice. "Thank you for explaining. I guess I'm still getting used to my new role here."

"Well, the good news is your essential role hasn't changed." Caster nodded at a passing colleague as they moved past a tastefully appointed atrium. "You're still in charge of ensuring your patient's physical welfare. You're to treat any illness or injury Jesstin incurs, to the best of your ability, in order to keep her properly healthy for the rigors of clinical trials. You're not to give her anything for pain, however."

"Nothing?"

"Strict unit policy. In fact, I want you to apply a small pain stimulus yourself, dear, during the first examination. No doubt you did this occasionally in the Civilian unit."

"Yes," Brenna said.

"While Jesstin should look to you as her medical advocate, she shouldn't be led to believe your role with her is entirely benevolent."

They had reached the doors leading to the laboratories and treatment rooms, where plush carpeting and carefully nurtured plants gave way to cold tile and disinfectant. A uniformed man with a studied bearing of command came through them briskly.

"General Lorber!" Caster lifted a hand to one breast.

"The good doctor." Lorber's eyes crinkled above his walrus mustache. "I hear our mighty Amazon is finally in residence!"

"That's right, General. In spite of the best efforts of some sadly deluded civilians, clinical trials will open right on schedule. Oh, I'm so glad you stopped by." Caster beckoned to Brenna and put a hand on her shoulder. "I'd like to present our unit's new medical technician, who comes to us with the most glowing professional references imaginable. Brenna, General Lorber is the Clinic's Military liaison."

"Miss Brenna." Lorber's large freckled hand devoured Brenna's. "With a Clinic team of such breathless beauty, how can we fail?"

Caster tittered girlishly. "The General is our own Roman warrior, Brenna, surging into battle against the rapacious Amazons of old! We couldn't have a more valorous ally."

Lorber's fleshy thumb drew lazy circles over Brenna's knuckles. She smiled up at him politely and slowly tightened her grip until he stopped. "It's an honor, sir."

"If you have a moment, General, I'd love to show you our latest estimates on the value of Tristaine's timber rights." Caster bestowed a parting smile on Brenna. "Run along and see to our illustrious patient, dear. And remember, I want you to feel free to come to me at any time, yes?"

Brenna watched the flirtatious brush of Caster's hand on the General's arm as they strolled back toward her office. She noted the distinguished Roman warrior avoided her eyes. She started to push through the double doors, then reversed herself and took a detour to the staff lounge. She checked to make sure she was alone, then opened her locker and pulled out a small silver flask.

She tipped it twice, whispering invectives. That brief lapse of professionalism worried her. Angering a General was simple stupidity. She couldn't let emotion goad her here. Her job was keeping her patient healthy, then cashing paychecks from the most prestigious research facility in the City. She would not make waves.

When Brenna pushed the heavy door of the detention cell open, she was relieved to note some improvement. While still cool, the cell's temperature was bearable. The prisoner lay quietly under the blanket, but she opened those disconcerting eyes when Brenna approached her.

"What do you say we start again?" She folded her hands behind her. "I'm Brenna, I'm Clinic staff. I'm going to take care of your health needs during the research study and be your medical advocate while you're in clinical trials. Remember that I have the authority to discipline or disable you at any time, if necessary. Understood?"

Jess swallowed. "Would this be a Military study or Civilian?"

Brenna heard the dryness in her throat, and she lifted a blue decanter of water and fit the bendable straw between Jess's lips. "This is the Military Research unit."

For a moment Jess was still, and then she pulled hard on the straw. The cool water sluiced down her sandpapered throat in a welcome flood, but she hardly tasted it. She would have preferred organ harvesting or the morgue to this. A Civilian study would probably kill her too, eventually, but Military research meant the Feds planned to use her against Tristaine.

"Caster is the scientist in charge of your project. She'll explain everything you need to know later." Brenna replaced the decanter on the table, and her voice took on a practiced, soothing cadence. "You just need to concentrate on following directions, Jesstin, and obeying rules, and you'll be fine. All that clear?"

"Clear," Jess said. She smelled whiskey. Wonderful. Clinical trials, Military research, and a Government pixie with a fondness for spirits and access to long needles. The luck of Tristaine's women hadn't turned yet.

"Also," Brenna rummaged in the pocket of her lab coat, frowning again, "I should have read this to you earlier." She pulled out an index card. "'Jesstin, your transfer to this medical facility was arranged under conditions of highest security. Be aware that armed peace officers—'" Brenna scowled and glanced up. "They mean orderlies with guns. 'That armed peace officers, stationed throughout the Clinic at all times, will ensure your compliance with unit rules.'"

She pushed the card back in her pocket. "It goes on like that for a while. Translated, you can rebel or try to escape if you wish, but someone will shoot you if you do."

Jess filed away Brenna's apparent distaste for this edict for future reference. A medical advocate must not rank highly enough in the hierarchy to know that the Feds had assured her compliance above and beyond the firepower of Clinic staff. She had little doubt that Camryn and Kyla would pay the price for any resistance she might offer.

"I need to patch you up." Brenna surveyed Jess critically. "Save us both time. Tell me where you're hurt."

"My head stings." Jess thought about it. "My side hurts. Other than that, cuts and bruises."

Brenna unbuttoned Jess's shirt and spread the black cloth apart. At first she thought the mark high on Jess's left shoulder was a deep bruise; then the intricate swirls of color asserted themselves into a complex design.

"Is this a tattoo? I've never seen one."

"It's a clan marking. It identifies my guild and the crest of my home village." Jess had seen her glyph inspire the same wonder in jaded Prison guards that softened Brenna's features now. In a society so threatened by individual expression that most forms of commercial art were illegal, the work of Tristaine's glyph-painters seemed magical. All but unreadable to City dwellers, the small circular etching of an arrow in flight marked Jess as a warrior, and the dancing stars formed a constellation signifying her Amazon heritage.

"It's beautiful," Brenna murmured.

"Thank you," Jess said simply. "I think so, too."

Brenna forced her eyes away from the glyph. Standing on her tiptoes and leaning over, she spotted a thunderhead bruise low on her patient's right side and drew in a breath. "That's got to hurt like hell, Jesstin. You might have a few cracked ribs."

"Don't think so."

"Well, I've got to be sure." Brenna straightened and regarded Jess. "I'll have to examine that bruised area and decide if you need X-rays. That's going to be painful. And I need to stitch the cut on your head." She paused. "You were right about analgesics, Jesstin. I can't give you any."

"Brenna?" Jess squinted up at her. "Just curious. How in blazes did you end up here?"

"What do you mean?"

"You don't seem to enjoy inflicting pain. I'm trying, but I can't see you as the bloodthirsty type." Jess's brogue deepened when she was tired, and she was starting to twirl her *r*'s.

"I'm a certified medical technician, Jesstin. I may be new to this particular unit, but I've seen my fair share of gore. Don't worry. I'm no green nurse's aide."

"You're a kid." Jess closed her eyes wearily. "You're probably a capable medic, lass, but how you got assigned to a gruesome outfit like Military Research—"

Brenna laid the flat of her hand over the bruise on the prisoner's ribs and pressed, gently but deliberately. Jess stiffened hard in her restraints.

"Okay." Brenna cleared her throat again. "Now you know I'm not just a capable medic. I'm also capable of correcting you if I have to." She folded her arms tensely. "Look, I'm required to apply a pain stimulus like that with a new patient. That makes it clear that I'll do what I—"

"Clear," Jess gasped.

Brenna waited uneasily until her patient was able to lie flat again in the restrainer.

Then she pushed up the sleeves of her coat, as if to reset her professional mode. "The other unit I was assigned to in the Clinic didn't do Military research, Jesstin. But we did lots of Civilian projects there, and I've worked with a dozen prisoners. Some of my patients did well, and they were released. Some of them wouldn't cooperate, and they went back to Prison."

Jess studied her, the pain still pounding in her side, and wondered if this girl really believed that release was an option in her case.

Brenna shrugged, her face impassive. "It didn't matter to me, my pay was the same. So don't push me, okay?"

Neither of them spoke while Brenna deftly stitched the cut above Jess's brow. She knew her fingers were cold on the rugged face, in spite of the restored warmth in the cell. She'd never stitched anyone without at least a numbing spray, and she found her patient's utter stillness beneath the fiery needle unnerving. However, her stitches were characteristically neat and even. She held herself to high standards when it came to patient care.

She moved to the other side of the recliner and used her palms and the flats of her fingers to detect any sign of fracture in the prisoner's ribs. She found none. Brenna applied salve and bandages as needed. Then she wrote clinical notes on the clipboard for some time while Jess dozed beneath the blanket.

Brenna brushed one hand through her bangs and noticed she'd gotten a smudge of blood on the corner of the blue intake form. She slapped down her pen in annoyance and went to the sink. She didn't realize her hands were trembling until she held them beneath the water, and she thought longingly of the flask in her locker.

She took a white cloth and folded it. Her patient was still shivering, from exhaustion and pain now rather than cold. Brenna patted the beaded sweat off Jess's forehead with the cloth and summarized her clinical impressions.

Jesstin of Tristaine was a slightly malnourished Caucasian female in her late twenties. She was in surprisingly good health and obviously was fit and physically active before her incarceration. To say the least, Brenna thought. She looked as strong as a horse. Her shoulders were broad, and according to her orders, her powerful arms and legs required constant restraint. She might have been sentenced to field work at the Prison, judging by the healing scratches on her long fingers.

Brenna unsnapped Jess's shirt again and patted the cloth over her throat before moving it over her stomach and sides, studiously avoiding the firm, pale breasts.

Jess lay quietly under her skillful ministrations. The feather-soft brush of Brenna's fingers soothed her at first. Then Jess became aware of the persistent tightening of her nipples. A wry smile curved her cracked lips. She would have sworn Prison life had banished all trace of her libido. She supposed she had Gaia to thank for the durability of Amazon lust.

"I'll tell you a secret of the medic's trade, Jesstin." Brenna ran the soft cloth down each muscled arm. "If you know how, and when, to administer pain, and your patient knows you're willing to, then you don't have to do it very often. Makes life more pleasant for both of us."

"Did you learn that bit of wisdom from this Caster, Brenna?" Jess's brogue softened the words. "That's the strategy of a bully, not a healer."

Brenna stared at her, but she saw another small tightening around Jess's eyes as pain flickered through her again, and she let the comment pass. A few minutes later she folded the cloth. "All right, Jesstin, you're patched for the night. Think you can sleep?"

"Sure." Jess shifted stiffly on the padded recliner, and another shadow of pain crossed her face.

Brenna studied her patient pensively. She flicked off the floodlight above them, plunging the cell into blue-hued darkness. Her searching fingers touched Jess's bare shoulder, then slid gently beneath her hair. She cupped the strong neck, noting the velvet-sheathed tension thrumming in her palm. She began working the tight muscles with strong fingers, closing her own eyes in order to concentrate.

"You're like me," she said. "We carry all our tension in our shoulders and neck. My little sister can put me to sleep in ten minutes doing this. Try to relax, Jess."

She probed the steely muscles silently for a while.

Jess remembered Kyla's cool hands on her back. Every night, in spite of a punishing shift in the Prison's kitchens, the young redhead spent hours on her and Camryn, kneading the ache from their locked muscles. Shann called Kyla her best student in the healing art of touch. Jess let the darkness hide the welling in her eyes.

"Listen." Brenna kept her voice low. "Your chart says you've got nothing but physical therapy for the next week. Caster wants to build your strength for the clinical trials. That means bed rest, decent meals, light exercise when you're ready for it…"

Brenna heard a light, buzzing snore in the darkness. She smiled and edged her hand carefully from beneath Jess's thick hair. She smoothed a stray lock off the sleeping woman's brow, sifting its softness through her fingers.

"I'm so good," she murmured.

CHAPTER TWO

They used to lop off one breast, so they could draw a
bow to shoot arrows in battles with the Greeks." Dugan
leaned on hairy forearms crossed on the circular desk next to the
staff locker room.

Brenna's Amazon patient was hot gossip, particularly
among the male orderlies. Morning shift change consisted of
little else. The three men had already seen Brenna, so it was too
late to avoid them. She continued her trek behind the desk to
retrieve Jesstin's chart.

"Amazons were Greeks," the big, pock-faced man slouched
next to Dugan corrected.

Jodoch was a recent addition to Clinic staff, and Brenna
hadn't met him formally, but his association with Dugan left her
less than eager to make his acquaintance.

"Modern Amazons don't do that." Dugan tipped a toothpick
at Jodoch. "Lop off a breast, judging by the cleavage on this one.
Hell, judging by the cleavage on this one, I wouldn't mind if they
hauled the rest of those renegade banshees down here."

"Even the dusky ones, stud?" The third orderly, Karney,
yawned as he poured coffee from the staff urn. "I hear they've
got Amazons in all colors up there."

"We got dames in all colors down here too, Karney, which
is why we built separate boroughs for 'em. Once that bitch-nest
is wiped out, the duskies can be locked up in their own Prisons. If
those ditzy witches up there are dense enough to give the whole
race relations mess another try, we'll mow 'em down without

breaking a sweat. Homeland Security has taught us how to deal with perverts like this."

Brenna slipped Jess's file out of the locked metal bracket reserved for Military projects, actively avoiding Dugan's avid gaze. His muddy eyes followed her, as they often did, but she'd grown accustomed to ignoring him.

"It's all bullshit." Karney sipped his coffee and grimaced. "Amazons died out tons of generations ago. They're comic-book fodder now. Beats me why Caster's got her knickers in a knot over this invert."

"Well, but see there, that's more proof that big honey in there is an Amazon. The Amazons were all inverts, Karney. Ask Jodoch here. He has a permit to study history." Dugan nudged his friend, but his eyes were still on Brenna. "The real Amazons were dykes. Right, Miss Brenna? You think that's why the sainted Caster is so hot on this study?"

"Caster's got three kids," Karney scoffed, stirring the murky brew in a Styrofoam cup. "She's sure not inverted."

"Is she, Brenna?" Dugan grinned. "You can tell us."

"I'll let her know you're interested." Brenna kept her tone pleasantly bland. She ducked under the wooden flap of the desk and headed toward the gymnasium to check out equipment for Jess.

"She wants me," Dugan crooned, and Karney chuckled.

❖

Brenna's chart notes over the next week were encouraging. Jess's bruises bloomed to full glory, then began to fade. The cut on her head closed neatly, and she showed no signs of concussion. She regained full range of motion on her right side, so the bruised ribs were coming along well. Jess healed faster than anyone Brenna had ever tended.

The sun burned high and hot in a flawlessly blue sky. Brenna blinked sweat out of her eyes as they entered the arena grounds. She tossed one of the sleek quarterstaves she carried to Jess, who walked beside her and caught it neatly.

"Hey, this is beautiful." Jess balanced the staff in her hands with apparent pleasure, studying its carvings. "I haven't done staffwork in years. Are these yours?"

"Just this one is." Brenna twirled the unadorned quarterstaff in one hand. "I signed that one out, and it's a matchstick by comparison, so watch it."

They were both somewhat hindered by attire. By regulation, Jess could wear only the black shirt and trousers of the Prison population. Brenna could have opted for something with a little more protection, but in fairness she dressed in scrub greens when they drilled.

Jess's physical therapy had quickly moved beyond bed rest, stretching, and exercise machines. Brenna had allowed her to graduate to drilling in a small enclosed arena that separated the Clinic from the Prison.

Two orderlies, usually Dugan and Karney, were posted on the high walkway encircling the neat workout field. They lounged lazily against upright posts in the sun, their rifles slung over their shoulders, watching. They would have been skeptical if told the two women drilling below were virtually unaware of them.

"You anchor your right foot rather than your left on attack?" Jess parried a confident thrust from Brenna's staff.

"Yep, helps me build momentum before I strike." Brenna danced a little, watching Jess's center of balance to predict her next move.

She knew her small stature was deceptive, as anyone meeting her in a ring found out. She was quick, even with alcohol making its first inroads in her fitness. And her compact, sturdy body was well proportioned. She still trained regularly, even in days clouded by a mind-numbing hangover, and she was stronger and healthier than she had any right to be.

"So whenever you shift your weight to your right foot," Jess noted, "I know you're about to smack me from the left?"

Jess sounded so confident that it was doubly satisfying when she mistook Brenna's pivot, bobbed when she should have weaved, and would have received a nice clout in the stomach if Brenna hadn't pulled her strike.

Jess grinned as Brenna indulged in a fist-pumping victory dance. Lately, after these sessions in Jess's company, her cheeks carried a healthy flush and her eyes danced in a way they usually didn't.

"You do announce that thrust, Brenna. Decent feint, though. You're fast."

"Gracious of you to admit it, since I all but gutted ye." Brenna managed a teasing imitation of Jess's brogue, then looked past her, and lowered her staff.

A middle-aged woman in a white coat was making her way across the arena grounds toward them. She lifted a hand in greeting as she minced carefully over the uneven ground in her sensible heels.

"That's Caster," Brenna said, sotto voce. "Be respectful, Jess."

"So this is Jesstin." Smiling, the woman came up to Jess and rested a nicely manicured hand on her shoulder. Nearly as tall as Jess, Caster appraised her with keen clinical interest. "She's looking well, Brenna. You're doing a fine job preparing her for her trials."

"Thank you, Caster." Brenna adopted a tone that was a shade more formal than usual. "Yeah, she's coming along. She's not ready for clinical trials, yet. Maybe next week—"

"My name is Caster, Jesstin. I'm Clinic staff." The slender woman reached into the pocket of her pristine lab coat and pulled out something small and metallic. "I've heard that members of your tribe are marked with some mystical symbol of their clan. Is that it? This lovely tattoo?" She laid the tip of the instrument against the glyph on the swell of Jess's left shoulder and pressed a button. There was an ugly buzzing sound.

Jess grunted, spun tightly, and fell, clutching her arm.

Brenna started, then stared at Jess in shock. "What are you doing?"

"I'm demonstrating the new patient-control device we're introducing to the unit." Caster's voice was calm and richly feminine.

She stepped away from Jess and showed Brenna the stunner, a streamlined, gleaming stylus. "It gives off quite a charge, but it's adjustable. I gave Jesstin here a fairly large jolt just now. Quite painful, but no lasting tissue damage, and the pain and disorientation fade after a few minutes."

Brenna watched Jess climb back to her feet. Her face was chalk white, and her long legs were visibly trembling.

"Why was that necessary?" Brenna asked sharply.

"Well, let's consider our subject, Brenna." Caster studied Jess, who carefully kept her expression inscrutable.

This is a ripe one, Jess thought, drawing deep breaths to dissolve the spun glass webbing her mind. Her shoulder throbbed as if it had been kicked by an iron-shod horse. She watched Caster lift a pair of half-glasses, draped around her neck by a jeweled silver chain, and gesture with it as she spoke.

"Remember our discussion, dear, about how difficult Jesstin finds it to accept her status as a convicted criminal? Her Prison chart indicates she is highly contemptuous of all forms of legal authority. Given her flagrant and chronic flaunting of regulations, it seems it would be perfectly all right with our Amazon if we returned to the chaos of democratic rule! A reminder of the wisdom of compliance was in order. Don't you agree?"

An almost irresistible urge to go to Jess held Brenna silent.

Caster rested her hand on Brenna's tense arm. "And you should have some backup yourself, dear, if you're working with her alone."

"I don't think I'll need a stunner, Caster." Brenna swallowed. "She's been pretty cooperative."

"And I'm sure she'll continue to be, now." Caster smiled,

with a carnivorous flash of white teeth. She gestured at the staff Brenna held. "I didn't mean to interrupt your therapy session, Brenna. Please continue."

"We were finished," Brenna said quickly.

"Nonsense, it's not even noon. Pick up your weapon, Jesstin."

Jess thought sourly that she should have seen this coming. Put this cold City shrike in stiletto heels, and she was a bloody cartoon version of a dominatrix. She bent stiffly and retrieved the staff from the grass.

"Caster, even drilling with a quarterstaff can be dangerous, and Jesstin still looks pretty groggy." Brenna used her hands to decorate her words, an old habit when she was agitated. "Maybe you'd like to come back after our lunch break and watch us go hand-to-hand. That's really her specialty."

"Brenna, I realize you're not in on all the Military strategy involved in this." Caster turned Brenna aside and slipped an arm around her shoulders. "You know that Jesstin comes from a faction of mountain women—yes, some are calling them descendants of the semimythical Greek Amazons—who are notoriously resistant to any kind of outside intervention. In spite of numerous overtures and rather generous terms, they blatantly refuse the patronization of our City Government. We're beginning to fear that the women of Tristaine are far too stubborn to accept peaceful annexation. And unfortunately, dear, our subject is as obstinate as the rest of her clan."

Caster kept an eye on the prisoner as she spoke soothingly to Brenna. "We don't need more information about Tristaine, Brenna. We could get that at any time through the use of chemical interrogation. Our goal is to find out what it takes to break an Amazon's will to resist. Permanently, not the short-term submission we can easily elicit through torture."

Brenna tried to imagine what kind of force would be necessary to break this particular Amazon's will. She would have to watch it happen.

"'Defeat the civilian's resistant spirit,'" Caster quoted from a journal article of her own that Brenna recognized, "'and defeat civilian resistance!' Hopefully, through bloodless assimilation—without our Army having to reduce Jesstin's lovely mountain haven to ashes and rubble. I'm simplifying vastly, of course, but if we're to have any hope of annexing Tristaine without bloodshed—if we wish to assimilate, rather than annihilate, an entire primitive culture, then we must use Jesstin here to give us a formula for transforming a savage Amazon into a peaceful, law-abiding citizen."

Caster pressed Brenna's shoulders. "Jesstin still needs discipline, Brenna. Even after months in lockdown and regular beatings, she is much too headstrong. If she goes into clinicals like this, she may not even survive them! We really need your help with this. And your part starts today."

Questions Brenna knew she couldn't ask moved sluggishly through her mind. "You want us to drill?" she asked faintly. "Now?"

"I want you to fight now," Caster corrected. "Take her down, Brenna. Hard. Make her feel it. Quickly. The effects of the stunner won't last much longer."

"But—"

"Now, Brenna."

Jess couldn't hear the murmured conference, but she braced herself when Brenna turned back with her staff clenched tightly in both hands. She streaked forward and attacked with a sudden fusillade of strikes, and Jess back-stepped several yards before she was able to fend her off. She finally locked their staves together and heaved Brenna back to clear space between them.

"Jesstin, listen to me." Brenna's tone was low and urgent. "Just drop your guard. Take one strike, fast and neat, and go down."

Brenna's staff flew out of her stinging hands, propelled by a kick so fast it hardly registered. Ordinarily, a blow to the exposed throat would follow, but Jess was woozy, not crazy. She danced backward lightly and hovered on the balls of her feet.

Brenna moved almost as quickly as Jess had. Her sneakered foot swept out in a sharp kick that thudded into Jess's unprotected side with audible impact. Brenna was so astonished at her success that it took her a moment to realize she'd kicked Jess flush in her bruised ribs.

Jess dropped her staff and teetered, then went to her knees, folding over the pounding in her side. Brenna locked her own knees to block the instinct to go to her. Her heart was a timpani in her chest, and she felt a sudden roil of nausea.

"Nicely done, dear." Caster smiled approvingly at Brenna, then addressed the gasping prisoner. "Think of it this way, Jesstin. For the past week, you have experienced our City's benevolence in the person of your lovely medical advocate here. She has tended you, nourished you, and seen to your every need and comfort, yes? And in return, she has required only your obedience and compliance with simple rules. Now, my brawny friend, just as this slip of a girl struck you down without warning, so Tristaine should respect and fear the City's vast—"

"Save your benevolence for the men of your City, Cassie." Still clutching her side, Jess sat carefully back on her heels. She heard Brenna's quick warning breath and ignored it. "If the women down here keep escaping to the mountains to join us, their husbands will only have your frigid white butt to warm their beds."

Brenna was having trouble keeping any one thought in her mind right then, but she was practically certain Jess couldn't have spoken those words. Not in that husky, sensual, mocking drawl.

The elegant woman next to her became still, and Brenna's heart skipped another jagged beat. "Take this," Caster said.

Brenna looked down at the stunner Caster was pressing into her hand. "Y-you want me to use this on her? Now?"

"Unless you have a problem with my judgment." Caster's voice was mild, but her black eyes were flinty.

"I don't think I can do this."

"You can and you will. Whenever it's necessary." Caster leaned closer, and her minted breath blew in brief, hot bursts against Brenna's cheek. "You can go far in Military medical research, Brenna, with the right contacts. But I warn you, you must steel yourself to this sort of thing. You don't want to be limited to applying Band-Aids all of your life. Remember that there are a dozen applicants for every promotion at the Clinic. And none of those candidates are squeamish."

Brenna swallowed.

"Full intensity," Caster instructed.

Brenna met Jess's gaze. She adjusted the dial on the stunner with cold fingers. A moment passed.

"Come now." Caster sighed. "Full intensity is hardly more than the first jolt I gave Jesstin. In fact, it might be best to administer this one in precisely the same place. High on the left shoulder, please, over the tattoo. Since the first dose obviously had such little lasting effect."

"Jess," she whispered.

Jess was keenly aware of the rifles trained on her back from the guard posts and the banshee Caster's avid gaze. She sat motionless on her heels. "I can't help you with this, Bren."

Brenna stared at the stunner in her hand, then at the hard swell of Jess's shoulder. The swirling lines of the glyph were muted under a flushing circular burn. The tip of the stylus trembled as she rested it in place. She had no real choice. She could feel Jess's gaze on her face, but she didn't meet her eyes as she fingered the switch. The ugly buzzing sound barked again.

Pain blasted through Jess's arm and chest and up to her throat, locking out breath. To her disgust, a sick gray haze settled over her, and she realized she was passing out. Brenna rose and backed away from Jess as if she were a snake thrashing in the grass. Jess sprawled on her back and lay still.

"Thank you, Brenna." Caster clasped her slender hands behind her and looked down at the unconscious prisoner. "I think we'll give Jesstin some time to ponder her options. The fresh air out here will do her good." With a smile, she added, "Well, my young colleague, with one brief lapse, you've been most professional this morning. Now you're about to earn some lucrative overtime. I want you to stay here tonight."

Brenna was staring at Jess's motionless form through the heat waves blurring her vision, but she nodded.

"Have Jesstin tied down, just as she lies. She's to remain here until midnight." Caster ticked the points off on her long fingers. "Understood?"

"Midnight," Brenna repeated stupidly.

Caster nudged Jess's leg with her foot. "You can find some shade and get caught up with your paperwork. Be sure no one gives her water. Escort your patient to her cell after midnight. Patch her up as needed. Remember, nothing for pain. Then take off. With six hours of overtime on your clock."

Brenna shrugged and nodded, feeling like a child. Her thoughts were boiling.

A mechanical buzzing issued from the pocket of Caster's lab coat, and she pulled out a compact cell phone. "Yes? Hello?" Her face lit with pleasure, and she lowered her voice. "Robert? He did! Oh, darling, that's wonderful. Yes, steaks for dinner. Fire up the barbie, I'm on my way. Love you too."

She folded the small phone with a happy snap. "My oldest just won the freshman division of the All-City Science Fair. He worked so hard…dear, I do have to run. Please see to all this, yes?" Caster patted Brenna's cheek and strode off toward the arena gate, checking her watch.

Brenna looked up at the festering sun, and her throat went dry. Jess was going to lie under this for six hours. Then six hours more, in the chill of night. She took a tentative step forward and studied Jess's pale features, her dusky lashes still against the high cheek. Her breathing was normal now, and her color was coming back.

Brenna shook herself mentally, and her lips parted to

call Dugan and Karney down off the walkway. Then her breath trailed out of her. She knelt beside Jess and rested the backs of her fingers against her face.

"I didn't want this," she whispered. "Jesstin?"

If she wanted absolution, Jess couldn't provide it. She was deeply out. Brenna brushed some hair off Jess's damp forehead. Even senseless, she projected a nameless dignity. Her austere beauty only heightened the effect. She looked like a warrior, Brenna thought, a fallen warrior out of myth.

She rose quickly to her feet. "Karney, stay here. Watch her," she called. Targeting the exit opposite the one Caster had taken, she homed in on it, walking fast. "Dugan, bring restraints."

"Glad to," Dugan called back from the catwalk. "You'll join us again, won't you, Miss Brenna? Where you going?"

"Locker," Brenna snapped, and kept going.

❖

12:30 a.m.

Brenna paused outside the detention cell and stared at the steel paneling of the door. She had waited in a shadowed corner until she heard the fading echo of Dugan's voice and the jangling of Karney's keys as the two men strolled back toward the staff station. Brenna breathed into her palm and sniffed, then pushed the door open.

The brilliant lamp suspended over the restrainer flooded Jess's body with merciless light. Her black clothing was still covered with the dust of the arena grounds, and she was trembling slightly.

Brenna had endured the hours much as Jess had, in less physical discomfort, but equally robbed of the ability to act. She left her patient only twice, once while Dugan and Karney staked Jess to the ground, and again when they took her back to the cell. She emptied half the flask in her locker each time. And she was still dismally sober.

Brenna opened the small drawer on the supply counter and took out a chemical ice pack. "I know you're awake, Jesstin."

Jess opened her eyes.

"I'm going to put this on your side." Brenna flexed the ice pack to activate it.

She unbuttoned Jess's shirt and spread it open. Her patient's firm breasts and belly were strikingly pale against her scarlet throat and upper chest. Her collection of faded bruises was highlighted by a newly painful discoloration low on her right side.

Brenna laid the ice pack gently in place, and Jess started. Her breasts lifted with the motion, and Brenna averted her gaze quickly.

Jess's throat felt like it was stuffed with socks. "How 'bout some water?" she croaked.

"Not right now." Brenna raised her eyebrows in dismay. "No, I'm not withholding it. You just need to rest for a moment longer before you drink, if you want any of it to stay down."

Jess nodded. Her extraordinary eyes were dull.

Brenna moved closer and laid her palm lightly across the base of her throat. The flesh beneath her hand was flushed with sick heat, but even as she watched, gooseflesh rose on Jess's collarbones. Sunburn aside, she was wracked with chills. City nights were as cold this time of year as its days were hot, and Jess had been staked out there for nearly twelve hours.

Brenna picked up one of the medications she'd taken from the dispensary and pressed a small amount of ointment into her hands.

"Jess, you're a little dehydrated." She controlled her voice, keeping it low and calm. "We need to push fluids as soon as we can and get your body temperature back to normal. Meanwhile, this cream is pretty good for sunburn." She hesitated. "I know you're tender. I'll be careful."

Brenna settled her palms on Jess's shoulders, avoiding the angry burn left by the stunner, and began to massage the cream into her reddened arms with gentle circular strokes.

Jess let her eyes focus blankly on a far wall and willed herself to relax under the soothing touch. She felt her nipples harden again and cursed silently. It was happening now whenever Brenna touched her. It didn't matter where. Her damn carnal urges were getting as rebellious as her tear ducts.

"You were a bloody idiot today, Jess." Brenna knew what she wanted to say. She'd had half the day and night to gather her thoughts. "You provoked that second stunner hit. Caster was within protocol to order it."

Jess said nothing. Brenna dabbed more cream into her palm.

"What happened afterwards," Brenna's fingers were light on Jess's forearms, "tying you out there all afternoon...I know that was harsh. I'm not disagreeing with Caster, but it was a... very strong intervention." She paused. "I'm sorry I had to hurt you."

Jess's eyes drifted shut under the pleasant stroking. "It wasn't your call, Bren." Her shoulder was killing her, and her side hurt. Even more than strictly merited, she thought, until she remembered who kicked it.

The heat of the sun had been punishing, and so was the abrupt chill that descended with dusk. But the Prison had offered far more torturous responses to insubordination. Stars filled the sky above Jess as night fell, refreshing her spirit as pleasantly as water would have slaked her thirst. Her very skin soaked up the faint starlight, parched after weeks behind stone walls.

Brenna supported Jess's head as she sipped water from the blue decanter. Those same stars look down tonight on Tristaine, she thought, holding the water in her mouth to savor its cool promise. Tears might have come, if she had been alone.

Brenna started to speak, stopped, then asked, "Jesstin, why were you sent to Prison?"

Jess pulled herself from her thoughts with effort. "They don't put that detail in patient charts, then?"

"No. Just a statement regarding the life sentence, but not

what it's for. We're supposed to assume everyone is dangerous."

"According to your Federal Tribunal, you're wise to abide by that assumption, lass. I was convicted of killing two women."

Brenna's hands stilled. "And you didn't do it," she said tonelessly.

Jess was silent for a moment. "I was there when they were shot," she said finally. "And I couldn't stop it. It feels like the same thing."

"What's that supposed to mean?"

Jess summoned the last of her energies and ordered her thoughts. She tried not to hope for much. "Your Government considered one of those women a threat, Brenna. Dyan. She sat on Tristaine's high council. So did I. Dyan was the leader of our warriors' guild, our fighting force."

Brenna listened, closing Jess's shirt.

"An Army squad found Dyan on a night patrol, but she wasn't alone. I was with her, and so was a young girl named Lauren. Dyan and Lauren were shot. I was arrested and charged with their murders."

Jess wasn't watching Brenna's eyes anymore. Too many nightmares replayed behind her own. "A Federal tribunal found me guilty in less than an hour."

"So Government troops shot two women on your high council," Brenna repeated slowly, "and framed you for it."

"Lauren wasn't on Tristaine's council." Jess shivered. "She was a kid. She just got in the way that night."

"Jesstin, make sense. Why would they do such a thing?" There was a strained note in Brenna's voice. "How could the Army justify—?"

"Seven of our grandmothers founded Tristaine, Brenna, generations ago. Refugees from the City. Today there are six hundred of us. Your women here are defecting in droves, lass. More come to us every day, from every borough, as rumors of Tristaine spread. And their daughters will find us too, in their time."

"Wait. Just wait. The Army is more than capable of bombing Tristaine to dust, Jesstin. Why would a Government that's trying to preserve your village sink to assassinating children?"

"Think, Brenna." Jess struggled against a rising need to convince this girl. "Your Government isn't interested in protecting Tristaine's heritage. There's only one reason the Army has spared us so far. If they wipe us out, we become legend. We've taken root in the public imagination, lass. Tristaine would be remembered as home to hundreds of martyrs. Movements have been launched on less. Your Government can't abide—"

"It's not my Government," Brenna said evenly. "The Government I know doesn't ambush innocent women in the middle of the night."

"Dyan was dangerous. They were right about that." Jess felt the sludge of hopelessness fill her. Brenna's confusion leaned toward skepticism. It was all over her face. "She was brilliant, and she knew how to fight. She would never have allowed Tristaine to be assimilated. They thought they could kill the snake by cutting off its head."

"Enough, Jess. I shouldn't have asked. Just rest for a moment." Brenna went to the sink and washed her hands, grateful for the distracting sound of the tinny water rushing from the tap. There were reasons medical staff weren't told about a prisoner's criminal record. What had she expected? Candor? An admission of guilt? Why should a dark conspiracy theory surprise her? She turned off the water with a wrench of the spigot.

She busied herself with a tray of medications from the Clinic pharmacy. She didn't see the labels on the small glass bottles until she made herself focus. Then she lifted one and read it, frowning.

"This isn't what I ordered." Brenna turned to see Jess regarding her. "It's an antiseptic for your arm. Your shoulder."

She showed Jess the small bottle. Jess eyed the label politely, then arched one dark brow.

"Sorry." Brenna smiled uneasily. "It's tecathenese. It's

very potent. It'll do the job, I guess, but there's at least a dozen other antiseptics I'd rather use." She paused as a wave of bleak resignation ghosted across Jess's features. "It's going to sting like hell."

Jess sighed. She was sick of being tortured by little girls, even conflicted ones. "Thanks for warning me. It helps, sometimes, if I can brace myself a bit."

"Does it?" Brenna asked softly. "Most people are the exact opposite, I've noticed. You wouldn't think so, but being surprised by pain is actually less traumatic than—" She made herself stop babbling and saturated a sterilized cloth with the astringent liquid.

She bent over Jess, and the dark head jerked infinitesimally away from her hand a fraction of an inch. Brenna accepted the flinch for what it was, without comment, and felt another stone lodge in her belly. She remembered her early days of training, before her transfer to the Federal program, when the guiding principle was to do no harm. She focused on the burns left by the stunner on Jess's shoulder.

They were not especially ugly wounds, but Brenna felt her throat tighten again when she saw the beautiful emblem of Jess's clan obscured by blisters and some bruising in an area about the size of a quarter. The skin around it looked flushed and tender.

"Your type of skin doesn't scar easily, Jess. The design should be clear again when this heals." She folded the dripping cloth in half and laid it on the marks.

Jess's assaulted nerves awoke with a vengeance. True to its reputation, the tecathenese was as scathing as acid. She jerked her head off the padded surface of the chair and clenched her fists in the restraints.

"Hey," Brenna said sharply. She pressed a hand to her waist. "Sorry, you startled me."

"Bracing myself didn't work," Jess gasped.

Brenna waited, wanting a drink so badly she trembled. When her patient's breathing returned to normal, she made herself take a clinical look at the wound. "I think I got it well covered. We'll let it air tonight. I'll bandage it in the morning."

She pulled the white cotton blanket over Jess's chest and then clicked off the overhead floodlight. Half-blinded, Brenna made her way around the bed and moved toward the door. The weary voice behind her stopped her, but only briefly.

"Do you know the next protocol, Brenna?"

"No." Brenna didn't, and she didn't want to. The next protocol was where it bloody well belonged, several flasks and dreamless hours away. "Get some sleep, Jesstin."

CHAPTER THREE

The answering machine was just ending its metallic greeting as Brenna keyed open her door. She wrestled the two slender, brown-bagged bottles to her kitchen counter, but not with any real haste. The skree of the recording signal skewered her aching temples. She took one of the bottles with her and settled on the couch.

"Hey. This is your pregnant sister. I know you're home, you're always home. You need to let me know if you think you'll make it to this barbecue or not. Matt's gonna invite his friend Sheila, but only if you come. She's gorgeous, by the way. I don't want Matthew to risk poisoning her with his toxic chili sauce unless there's a good medic around."

There was a pause, and Brenna rested her head on the back of the couch, rolling the acid flood of vodka over her tongue. Her eyes closed at the wistful note in Samantha's voice.

"Bree, it's been a while. We said nothing would change, right? You know Matt's crazy about you. You can come over anytime. Like, every day would be nice, once this kid is born. We'll always get you home by curfew. Is that what you're worried about?"

"Ah, Sammy," Brenna sighed.

"So pick up a phone already." Her sister's tone lightened. "We owe you a steak for helping us fill out all those pregnancy permits. Hey, you want us to invite your new boss to the barbecue too? We saw a profile of her on the news last week, and she looks really...well, shrewish, frankly, Bree, no offense. We'll give her extra chili sauce. You haven't told me anything about your new unit. Geez, it's been that long since we—"

The machine's rude screech cut off the sweet music of Samantha's voice and left Brenna in the ticking silence of her small studio.

It was standard Government issue, a well-constructed but strictly functional cubicle. She had made a halfhearted gesture toward decorating when she first moved in, but the laws governing the production of art limited consumers to a depressingly drab roster of generic prints and paintings. Samantha kept bringing her houseplants, but they all gave up the ghost eventually because Brenna forgot to water them.

The wall above her desk, the focus of the room, was adorned only with the neat, framed diplomas and certificates that marked her professional milestones. In contrast to the rest of the studio, which featured a neglectful haze of dust, Brenna's desk was pristine and gleaming.

She let out a shaking breath and sank lower on the couch, willing her shoulders to relax. She passed more of her nights here, now, on the sagging comfort of the sofa and with the numbing solace of liquor, in the six months since her assignment to the Clinic. It didn't look like her first patient in the Military unit would change that pattern much, but she found it difficult to care.

Brenna swirled the drink in its juice glass, then downed it and let her mind drift. She thought of riding, oddly enough. Not riding itself, at first. A City girl, she'd only seen pictures of horses.

A brown mare, nuzzling its spindle-legged foal in the confines of a fenced corral. The warm breath of mother and child puffed twin plumes of steam in the cold morning air. Then the mare heard the trumpeting call of a stallion, and her head rose sharply, ears pricking. She dipped her muzzle to her foal in farewell, then loped across the corral and soared over the splintering four-rail fence. Her pounding hooves brought her closer to the beautiful black horse, prancing in a distant meadow.

Then Brenna was astride the stallion, riding it, feeling the shimmering power of the beast between her thighs. They flew down the twisting trail of a mountain path, breathing in the clean scent of pine as one creature. Brenna's hands were light on the stallion's pistoning neck, and her heart filled with such alien joy that her eyes, closed against the worn fabric of the couch, brimmed with tears.

The spear came from nowhere, plunging deep into the black horse's massive chest. The beautiful animal stumbled as its heart was impaled by the iron point—and seemingly Brenna's heart as well. She sobbed once, bereft, and then the stallion staggered, pitching her over its head toward the crumbling edge of a stone bluff…

A horrible buzzing woke Brenna. The ringer on her phone was set at high volume, should something happen with a patient in the night. Part of Brenna's sludged mind recognized that night had apparently come and gone, but mostly it focused on silencing the cranium-rattling telephone. She lurched across the studio and snatched the receiver from its cradle.

"Brenna?" It was Charlotte's nasal, faintly disapproving voice. Caster's secretary was all but universally hated, and calls like this were why. "You do realize rounds are half over, don't you? It's almost ten o'clock."

Brenna squinted at the wall clock over the phone. "I meant to call in, Charlotte. Please give my apologies to Caster, but I've been hit with a nightmare virus or something—"

"Just a moment, please." There was the muted tapping of computer keys, and Brenna imagined an alley cat stalking haughtily across her nerve endings. "Brenna? Excuse me, but are you aware that you've used…more than half of your annual leave, in the twenty-six weeks you've been with us? Caster tries to be flexible with her staff, but…"

Brenna felt an unwilling flicker of fear in her gut, as well as irritation. Her absences would be tracked carefully from now on. Her hand drifted to her throat. She remembered the feel of Jess's strong neck cupped in her palm, and she shuddered. She couldn't go in today.

"Brenna?"

"Thank you, Charlotte. I'll keep it in mind." Brenna summoned the wettest, most snot-filled sneeze ever sprayed into any mouthpiece. "Please tell Caster I'll be in tomorrow."

She fumbled the receiver back in its bracket and sank onto the bar stool next to the phone. Her reflection in the side of a silver kettle on the stove was thankfully distorted. Her skin held a gray pallor, and her short hair stood up in haphazard spikes.

Brenna rested her head on her arms as a thumping headache and queasiness asserted themselves. She thought of the medicated patches in the bathroom cabinet. She could stick one on her arm and banish her misery in minutes. She wondered who had bandaged Jesstin's shoulder that morning before she faced another day without painkillers.

She banished the thought quickly and went to hunt through the sofa cushions for her juice glass.

❖

Brenna pushed up the sleeves of her white coat, backed open the door to the detention cell, and came to a startled halt. Jess was sitting upright on the side of the recliner, unrestrained and fully dressed in fresh Prison blacks. Brenna fumbled for the stunner clipped to her belt, then slipped her hand into her coat pocket to disguise the motion.

"Your witch doctor opted to spring me." Jess's low voice was toneless as she shucked up one boot. "She figures you'll use that thing if you have to."

"I will." Among a dozen other emotions, Brenna felt muted relief. "How are you feeling, Jesstin?"

"I'm fine."

And her patient did look all right, physically. The thick layers of Jess's hair were clean and soft against her neck, and the sunburn had gentled to a golden bronze. Her shoulder was neatly bandaged, and she pulled on her other boot with no evident pain. Her angular features were expressionless, but virtually unmarked.

Brenna consciously did not flinch as Jess lifted herself off the restrainer. The Amazon moved slowly, as if to avoid alarming her.

"Caster was just here." Jess flipped her collar up beneath her hair. "We're expected to join her in the arena."

After a moment of silence, during which Brenna made no move toward the door, Jess lifted an eyebrow.

"Jesstin," Brenna began.

Jess waited.

"I'm Clinic staff. All right?" Brenna hadn't realized she would be making this speech, but she let it emerge, speaking slowly and clearly, as if to a dim child. "This is how I make my living. I'm alone. I pay all the bills. I've worked hard for what I have. Placements like this don't come along often, not in this economy."

Jess nodded.

"I'm just saying I'll do what's necessary, Jess." Brenna lowered her voice. "I may not like an order, but I'll carry it out. I don't have a choice."

"No need to apologize."

"This isn't an apology." Brenna furrowed her brow. "I don't owe you an explanation. I just wanted to tell you what to expect, before we go out. And just…that I'm glad you're all right."

"Thank you."

"Okay." She turned toward the door.

"Bren," Jess said softly. "In Tristaine, there are always choices."

Brenna opened the cell door and waited for the prisoner to precede her.

❖

Brenna's nerves tightened again as soon as they entered the arena. Seven rather large men, dressed in fighting gear—helmets and body pads—stood clustered at one end of the workout grounds. They were Clinic orderlies, most of them. Brenna recognized Dugan and a few others from day shift. The rest wore the gray uniforms of the guards in the adjoining Prison.

As soon as Caster saw Brenna and Jess come through the gate, she waved them nearer with her clipboard. "Here they are, at last. Is the camera ready, Stuart?"

"Ready." A bespectacled assistant from Caster's unit squinted into a video camera mounted on a tripod.

"Glad to have you with us again, Brenna. Jesstin, I think you know the drill here." Caster gestured toward the center of the arena. "You're to meet these fighters in hand-to-hand combat, yes?"

"Wait a minute." Brenna looked from Jess to the waiting men. "She's fighting them?"

"She's going to take them all on," Caster confirmed. "One at a time, to begin with. Mr. Jodoch, are you ready?"

The big acne-scarred orderly lifted a hand and trotted forward. He carried a small club studded with spikes.

"Hold it. I don't like this." Brenna put out an arm and stopped Jess. "That guy's armed. Doesn't she get a weapon?"

"No, Brenna. Jesstin's specialty is openhanded fighting." Caster gave her a chiding look. "If you'd been at yesterday's briefing, dear, you'd be on the same page with all this. Just a minute, Jesstin."

Jess had moved past Brenna's arm and started toward the fighting field. She looked back.

"Shirt off, please," Caster called.

A sardonic expression crossed Jess's face, but she seemed neither rattled nor surprised. She unsnapped her shirt and slipped it off her wide shoulders, baring her breasts. Their paleness contrasted vividly with her tanned belly and throat.

"Partial nudity makes female subjects feel more vulnerable," Caster instructed Brenna. "Besides, it's much more authentic for an Amazon, yes?"

One of the orderlies hooted obediently, but Jess ignored him. She tossed her shirt to the grass and walked toward Jodoch again, rolling her injured shoulder to loosen it, apparently relaxed with fighting shirtless.

"I believe we're ready, Stuart!" Caster brushed a leaf from the lapel of her white coat, then gave her sprayed coiffure a careful pat. She cleared her throat and faced the video camera with a tight smile.

"Madam Undersecretary, Dr. Aldin, General Lorber... ladies and gentlemen. Good morning." Caster's dulcet voice was formal as she addressed the lens. "The date you see below this frame marks the opening of clinical trials for Military Research Study T-714, Phase One. Please take a moment to consult our prospectus."

Caster paused, smiling. "As you read along, you will see that Phase One of our study involves establishing a baseline of resistant behavior in our test subject. Jesstin?" Caster gestured toward the center of the arena.

Jess watched the camera pan toward her and understood why she'd been ordered to remove her shirt. A half-naked barbarian was both titillating and easier to objectify. She continued the sequence of breathing rituals that prepared her to fight.

"As you can see, our Tristainian subject projects quite an intimidating presence." Caster tapped Stuart to keep the frame focused on Jess as she continued. "Jesstin is a valued member of Tristaine's elite warrior guild! She is honored among her violent kindred for her fighting prowess and her fearlessness in battle."

Jess wished she could fart loud enough to be heard on the tape. It was what Dyan would do. Dyan would focus on her breathing, Shann's voice corrected her silently.

"For the gentle layfolk on our panel," Caster smiled again, "Phase One of our study will demonstrate that brute force alone is unlikely to compel an Amazon to accept defeat. We will test this hypothesis with a series of trials, and the protocol is simplicity itself. Today, as in all of these sessions, Jesstin can end her punishment at any time, simply by agreeing to sign a statement renouncing Tristaine."

Jess glanced at Brenna, who was skimming forms on the clipboard with an intense frown.

"Please see section A-5 of the prospectus for a copy of the renunciation," Caster added. She raised her voice. "All right, Mr. Jodoch!"

Jess let her attacker advance, studying his body and lumbering gait methodically. As always at the opening of a fight, Dyan's voice guided her. Camryn, Jess remembered randomly, actually nodded in moments like this in drills, agreeing with her mentor's silent instruction. It wasn't a distraction, thinking of Cam and Kyla now, or of Dyan and Shann. Jess was fighting for her adanin, and their faces strengthened her.

Jodoch lost the mace after his first ineffectual swing. He was a powerfully built man, but he was no warrior. Jess's knee in his soft belly slowed him down. The side of her wrist to the back of his neck dropped him. She stood brushing the grass from her hands, breathing easily, as the orderly got to his feet.

Brenna's neck ached with tension as she scribbled a quick summary on the clipboard, not hearing the friendly jeers of the other men as Jodoch limped back to them.

"Well, that was hardly the bloodbath I almost hoped for!" Caster folded her arms and gave Brenna a conspiratorial nudge. "Has your tender care turned our studly Amazon into a pacifist, dear?"

"She's fighting without harm." Brenna shifted away from

Caster. "It's how we drill. It's a technique that limits the injury inflicted on an opponent."

"Ah. Jesstin's only prudent choice, given her status."

"Yes." Brenna knew very well that the men Jess faced fought under no such restraint. The next man, Karney, was just as big as Jodoch, and more experienced. He wielded a dagger. Jess disarmed and pinned him, but he scored a shallow cut across the top of her chest before she did. High whistles rose among the men at this first drawing of blood, and Brenna gripped the clipboard.

"You'll note that after finishing off one challenger, Jesstin immediately turns to meet the next." There was a note of pride in Caster's narration. "Our own fine Clinic staff can't quite claim that level of endurance." She called teasingly, "Correct, Mr. Jodoch? I see you're still a bit winded!"

Brenna's lips were sore because she kept scrubbing them with her hand—a sign her younger sister would recognize as craving for a drink. She didn't know the third orderly who jogged out to face Jess. They were becoming interchangeable in their pads and helmets, but he carried a standard issue Prison baton. He connected a few times before Jess took him out, including two solid blows to her lower back.

She's tiring, Brenna thought, she has to be. The Amazon was an excellent fighter, certainly the best she'd ever seen, but she was not superhuman. It took Jess longer to finish the fourth bout, with a man swinging a vigorous hand scythe.

When he finally limped off the field, Jess used the brief recovery time to store as much oxygen in her blood as possible. As she waited for her fifth opponent to emerge from the trio of padded men by the far wall, she admitted that soon the respites between matches wouldn't be enough. She didn't feel the pain of numerous minor strikes yet, but they were adding up. All Dyan would ask is that she fight well, Jess reminded herself, and accept defeat with honor. She could manage that.

"Ladies and gentlemen, difficult as it may be, try not to

get caught up in the excitement, drama, and age-old allure of the arena!" Caster paused while Stuart fumbled to focus the lens on her again. "We'll give Jesstin a moment to recover while we summarize our findings this morning. You'll note that, far from requesting an end to this trial, our warlike subject seems quite at ease in her natural habitat. Well, let's take Jesstin at her word and up the ante, shall we?" Caster turned and waved to the three men still standing. "All three of the rest of you, please!"

"Three at once?" Brenna's tone was sharper than she intended. "Why?"

Caster's sunny smile vanished. "Lower your voice, Brenna. That mike is sensitive." She clasped her arm to steer her away from the camera. "All of this was covered thoroughly in the briefing yesterday, dear, that you were apparently too ill to attend. However, I will repeat, just for you, that this trial is continuing because Jesstin has not yet conceded defeat. Do you have any clinical objections?"

"Well, Caster, yeah." Brenna tried for a light note while she watched the three men surround Jess. "We don't want to kill her, do we? On the first day?"

"Brenna, don't be dramatic." Caster's fingers tightened on her arm, but her voice was only gently chiding. "Clinic orderlies and Prison guards are hardly gladiator material. They won't kill Jesstin today, or even disable her. Phase One consists of at least three trials. Stop fretting, Brenna. Just observe."

The three remaining opponents formed a rough triangle around Jess, who waited, braced, her head turned slightly to detect any warning whisper of boots on grass. Her bare torso gleamed under the sun as she steadied her breathing. Red patches here and there stood out against her tanned skin, marking successful blows from earlier bouts. Blood glistened at the base of her throat from the dagger's cut.

One of the men she faced now held a net ready, another a quarterstaff, and the third, Dugan, a doubled length of thick chain. Jess brushed her sweat-soaked hair out of her eyes, amazed.

These City men fought like children, surrounding her efficiently, but dancing in place, waiting to attack one at a time. She thought, rather sourly, that she should feel gratified that witnessing four previous matches had instilled such caution in her opponents, but she knew their hesitation wouldn't last long. It didn't.

"Full force, please," Caster called. "Avoid the head, Mr. Dugan. I'm watching you!"

Sometime during the next fifteen minutes, Brenna realized that she was probably lucky to be alive. The drills she'd run with Jesstin the previous week had been child's play to the Amazon. Even fighting without harm, she was a blur of whirling kicks and expertly targeted strikes. In spite of Brenna's considerable hand-to-hand skills, Jess could have taken her out, fatally, at almost any time. And regardless of Caster's illusions, Brenna knew that Jesstin of Tristaine could have wiped the field with these men, if she were free to use real force.

The round lasted a long time. Too long. The three men couldn't quite pin Jess, and they couldn't keep her cornered for long, but they could and did overwhelm her whenever possible. Blood made a second appearance after Dugan slapped the chains across her upper back, digging shallow cuts.

Brenna scrubbed her hand across her mouth again, but made herself watch.

Jess found herself deep in the battle haze Dyan described so eloquently around Tristaine's storyfires. She didn't much like it there. She never had. Neither had Dyan, which was one reason she had been loved in Tristaine, as well as respected. The detached fury did feel familiar, though, and Jess was grateful for it now. It kept Kyla and Camryn clearly centered in her mind.

Then the man carrying the staff took a roundhouse swing and batted her in the gut. She grunted and dropped to her knees in the grass.

"Hold it!" Brenna's cry seemed to burst out of her. The men lowered their weapons, panting, and watched her stride toward them. "You three, back off!"

They stepped back obediently, even Dugan. Jess thought that was odd until she caught a glimpse of Brenna's fierce expression. Damned if the girl didn't look like an enraged Shann on the warpath.

Caster rolled her eyes and slapped the clipboard against her thigh, but she didn't stop her. "All right. Cut, Stuart."

Brenna dropped to her knees in front of Jess and eased her back into a sitting position as she pulled air into her lungs.

"Jesstin?" Brenna took her damp face in her hands. "Talk to me."

"Good call," Jess gasped. "I needed the break."

"Lean back. Let me see."

Jess rested back on her extended arms, and Brenna passed her hands carefully over the flat planes of her belly. "Does this hurt? Any tenderness? It looked like you were clubbed right in the liver."

"No, he just winded me."

"Jesstin." Brenna stared at the bleeding cut beneath Jess's throat. "All you have to do to end this is sign a form. Or just go down, but do one or the other!"

"I'll go down soon enough," Jess acknowledged.

Brenna gripped her arm tightly. "I know that," she snapped. "So does Caster! If you know it too, why drag it out?"

"All right, Brenna, please." Caster was tapping her pen against her board. "You—Mr. Jodoch? Are you functional again? And—I'm sorry—Karney? You are too? But Mr. Barbeler is nursing a broken hand. Well, the two of you, please join in again."

"Don't pull that macha Amazon crap now, Jesstin." Brenna's voice was strained. "Go down."

Jess said nothing, but put out an arm.

Brenna swallowed, then helped her to her feet. Then she left the fighting circle, and the five men surrounded the prisoner.

Jess steadied herself, nodded that she was ready, and they attacked. The break had helped her. She fought with a cool economy again, rationing her strength, keeping a steady eye on her closest opponent. She returned their blows in a controlled and violent dance that held its own alien beauty, and two of her opponents dropped quickly.

But her revival couldn't last, and Brenna knew it, even before Jess took Dugan's roundhouse right to the jaw and fell a second time.

Brenna turned to Caster. "Okay, stop the trial."

"What? Again?" Caster frowned. "Brenna, look, she's getting up."

"It doesn't matter. Stop the trial. Jesstin isn't going to give in today, Caster. They'll just keep beating her until she sustains a serious injury. That becomes more likely as she tires."

"Brenna—"

"I'm her medical advocate. I say she's had enough for today. That's my prerogative, and it's my call. Now stop the trial."

Caster let out a long breath, watching Jess sway on her feet. Karney clubbed her hard across the back, and she fell again.

"Caster!" Brenna's eyes snapped with angry light.

"All right. Stuart? Stop the tape." Caster folded the clipboard in one arm and clapped her hands. "Gentlemen, thank you for your assistance. That will be all for this morning."

Jess's first opponent, Jodoch, extended his large hand to the fallen Amazon. After a moment she accepted it and let him pull her to her feet.

"Brenna, perhaps you're right." Caster appraised her assistant. "It is the medical advocate's responsibility to protect the subject's physical welfare. I don't want you to think I doubt your professional judgment. And actually…this was a fair place to conclude this trial. We can call it a success."

"A success." Brenna watched Jess bend and rest her hands on her knees, her lean sides heaving as she pulled for air.

"Well, we wanted to establish a baseline," Caster explained. "We didn't force Jesstin to fight to complete exhaustion, but that's all right. We've documented her resistance. We know how far we can push her in one session and still keep her conscious. That's valuable information for future trials."

Brenna felt a cold dread snake through her. "She'll be doing this again?"

"Well, no, not this exact protocol. Really, Brenna, that briefing was important." Caster rummaged in the pocket of her lab coat and checked her pager. "Tsk. Wouldn't you think a man with two doctorates could look after two reasonably responsible youngsters for just one morning without constant guidance? The second trial isn't for a few days, Brenna. We'll give Jesstin adequate time to recuperate."

"Recuperate for what? What's the proto—?"

"Take our mighty warrior over there back to her cell, yes? It's all right to treat her injuries, Brenna, but remember, no analgesics."

Caster raised her voice as she followed the trailing orderlies out of the arena's enclosure. "Mr. Barbeler, I am so sorry about your hand! Let me make a quick call and I'll splint you myself."

The man named Barbeler didn't seem to feel Caster's sympathetic pat as she passed him. He stopped and looked back at Jess. He could have been just a big farm kid before he became a Prison guard. He stared at Jess, cradling his injured wrist in one freckled hand. Then he nodded at her before turning away, an oddly respectful bobbing of the head.

Jess lifted her chin slightly in response. Then she bent, stiffly, and tried to snag her black shirt off the grass with two fingers. Brenna was there in time to hand it to her. Jess blinked the sweat out of her eyes so she could see her. Brenna's lips seemed chafed and raw.

"I need to take a look at you." Brenna hovered as Jess painfully eased the shirt over her bare shoulders, then moved to adjust the fabric around her neck. "Can you make it to the detention wing?"

"I'm on my feet, Brenna," Jess said shortly.

She turned her head and spat red into the grass. When she

turned back, she moved her head too fast and caught a moment of dizziness. Brenna put her hands on her patient's chest to steady her, and their eyes met again.

Jess's awareness spiraled down to Brenna's soft hands bracing her and the shadowed eyes searching her battered face. She groaned inwardly. Amazon lust after battle was such a tired cliché. And she was such a tired Amazon.

It was like bracing a tree, Brenna thought. Winded, bloody and battered, gleaming with sweat, Jess towered over her like a cresting wave. She was stunned by an almost overpowering urge to slide her hands into Jess's open shirt and run her palms over the corded muscles of her back. Not to comfort her patient, but to find protection herself in the strength of those arms. Unsettled, Brenna dropped her hands and stepped back.

Jess started wearily toward the arena exit.

They were halfway across the field when they heard it, a distant, heavy tapping. It sounded like a block of wood hitting plastic, muted, but regular and insistent. Jess turned and looked toward the source of the sound, the Prison next door.

Brenna was focused entirely on getting her patient back to her cell before she had to call for a stretcher, but something in Jess's sudden stillness made her turn too. "What is it?"

She followed Jess's alert gaze toward the looming brick building at the outer perimeter of the Prison's electrified fence. The cinder-block wall was pocked with oblong windows, thick plates of glass laced with iron mesh. At the closest window, Brenna saw the outline of two figures—young women.

One of them, the taller one, raised a fist. The other, Brenna caught a flash of lush red hair, lifted her black prison shirt over her head and began a shimmying dance.

Brenna looked up at Jess and saw her tight smile before she turned and continued toward the exit. Her gaze shot back to the Prison window. The two figures had vanished. Brenna trotted a step to catch up with Jess.

"Brenna—"

"The sun was in my eyes," Brenna said. "I couldn't see through the glare."

Jess allowed herself a moment of relief.

Camryn and Kyla might indeed fail to survive their sojourn in the City, because if Jess ever saw them again, she was going to strangle them herself. She didn't want to hear about how light security was in the mess hall. That stunt had been both dangerous and pointless.

But seeing them again returned the steel to Jess's aching spine, at least until she was sure she had passed out of sight of the Prison wall. She made it back to the detention cell without resorting to the indignity of Brenna's support, but it was a long hike.

❖

Brenna flipped on the arc lamp over the restrainer and began setting out medical supplies. Jess limped to the sink and scrubbed her face and arms with cold water.

The silence was almost comfortable for a moment.

"Do you know if you're allergic to aneascin?" Brenna peered at an amber vial through the light. "I put in an order for some. It's less caustic than the tecathenese." Her tone held an appropriate note of light professional concern.

"Soap and water will do as well." Jess dried her face in a white towel. Most of the marks on her face had stopped bleeding. "You can go home, Brenna, if you want. There's nothing I can't take care of myself."

Brenna took the towel out of Jess's hands and tossed it on the sink. "I don't come and go at your behest, Jesstin. You know that."

She took her arm and drew her beneath the wash of light from the lamp. The bunched muscle beneath her fingers tightened, and Brenna touched the stunner at her belt. The impulse shamed her. Jess stood obediently in front of the restrainer while Brenna tilted her face to see the swelling capping one high cheek.

"That's going to be ugly in the morning," Brenna murmured.

She unsnapped Jess's shirt and spread it open, appalled. Jess's chest and stomach were covered with livid marks, most of them new, emerging bruises, but also some scrapes and cuts that still seeped blood.

Brenna studied the shallow, angry cut just above her collarbone and remembered the sun's flash on Karney's dagger. She touched the enflamed skin around the cut and looked up into Jess's eyes.

Jess entreated Gaia silently. Those accursed eyes were losing their clinical sheen. The girl looked weary and sad and afraid. Jess swallowed, hard. Luckily, a bad twinge of pain from her kidney broke the moment.

"What was that?" Brenna asked sharply as she helped her straighten.

"I think it was the second club strike," Jess stammered, gripping the small of her back.

Brenna began to peel the shirt off Jess's wide shoulders, but changed her mind and slipped her hands beneath it and around her waist instead. "I can tell more about this kind of injury by feel than by sight."

She moved her hands carefully beneath the black shirt and settled them on the warm planes of Jess's lower back. She pressed very gently. "Does this hurt?"

"Not much."

Brenna's hands moved higher. "How about here, does this?"

"No. Pain's fading."

Her hands moved again, and she had to step in closer to Jess to reach higher. She made the mistake of looking up into her eyes again, just as her palms cupped her shoulder blades.

"Does this hurt?" she whispered.

"No." Jess lifted her scratched hand slowly and placed it over Brenna's heart. "Does this hurt?"

Brenna stared at her, and she was lost.

They're going to kill me in the end, anyway, Jess rationalized. Her battered hand left Brenna's breast and rose to her chin. She bent her head and kissed her.

The full lips brushing warmly against Brenna's sent a painfully pleasant tingling through her blood. She leaned against the muscular body as the kiss deepened, and her hands crept up into Jess's hair.

Jess felt Brenna's firm breasts pillow beneath her own naked ones. Her tongue darted between her lips, and Jess sucked her, gently.

Jess had time to lift her head and release her when they heard the cell door open, and Brenna was able to step back out of her arms. That might have been enough. Given Jess's injuries, anyone else might have thought they were interrupting a medical exam. But Caster's eyes focused at once on the color filling her assistant's cheeks and the prisoner's prominent nipples.

"Excuse me, Brenna. I'm sorry to interrupt." Caster smiled, her heels clicking on the concrete floor as she slipped her clipboard onto the side table. "I thought you would have left by now. I came to put some tecathenese on that neck laceration, but I see you have things well in hand. Yes? So it might behoove us if I use this time instead to see if our Jesstin wants one more chance to avoid any further physical unpleasantries."

"Trials are over for the day, Caster." Brenna heard the tremor in her voice.

"Yes, dear, officially. But the quest for knowledge punches no time clock." Caster stood in front of Jess and looked at her body appraisingly. "Let's see, I need some small, insignificant wound…"

Brenna moved silently away from them. She stood near the sink and folded her arms.

Caster took the stunner from the pocket of her lab coat and rested the tip against the bleeding cut at the base of Jess's throat. Brenna wanted to close her eyes.

"Actually, this is too close to the heart to be entirely safe, Jesstin. Even at half intensity. Isn't there something you'd like to say to me?"

"Don't do it."

Caster's penciled eyebrows rose; then she looked back over her shoulder at Brenna and smiled. "You'll note that that was a command, Brenna, not an entreaty. Jesstin is forbidding me to stun her. Typical. Try again, Jesstin."

She tapped the cool steel of the stunner gently against the cut, smearing the shiny metallic surface with old blood.

Jess looked at her silently.

Brenna begged, "Say it, Jess."

"Come on now," Caster coaxed.

Tap, tap, tap.

"Just add that one, all-important word, Jesstin, and your command becomes a request. You know the word I mean. Every City child learns it in kindergarten. Don't do it…what?"

"Don't do it…bitch."

Brenna jerked her head away as the ugly snapping sound filled the cell.

CHAPTER FOUR

"Brenna? It's me."

She was swaddled in sweatshirts and two blankets, and she still couldn't get warm. Brenna burrowed deeper into the couch, shivering as the knock sounded again.

"I can stand out here all morning," the voice called from the concrete slab that comprised Brenna's front porch. "You know I'm not bragging, right? I'm threatening."

Go away, Sammy, Brenna thought.

"I went through your garbage. If you keep pretending you're not home when I come over, you gotta expect stuff like that." The muted worry in her sister's voice made her sound older than her twenty years. "How many bottles do you go through in a week now, Brenna?"

Must have been old garbage. Brenna had emptied the last bottle the night Jess fought in the arena and hadn't had a drop since. She thought the bouts of chills came from alcohol detox, and she was partially correct.

"Are you really going to make me stand out here on this stupid stoop? Me and your unborn niece or nephew?"

Her feet were the worst. They were ice. She dug them beneath the dusty cushions, hoping for a pocket of warmth. The unit was dark, the blinds closed against the morning sun. They had been closed for three days. Darkness helped her think.

"Bree, open the bloody door already!"

The light skewered Brenna's eyes as she unlatched the screen, and she retreated to the gloom of the studio. She could feel Sammy's eyes, the same shade of green as her own, though less guarded, burning a hole through the back of her robe. Her younger sister tossed her keys on a side table and made a frowning perusal of the cluttered unit.

"The tacky bitch who answers the phone at the Clinic said you've been out sick since Monday. So how sick?"

"It's just a bug, Sammy." Brenna sank back down into the sofa. "I'm sorry. I must have been dead to the world when you came over before."

"Must have been." Samantha rested her hand on her belly, which was just beginning to show the first sweet swell of growing life. Her fair skin was taking on the luminous quality common to new mothers, and Brenna felt her own face soften.

"You look beautiful, Sam."

"Yeah? You look like you haven't slept in a week."

Brenna had done little else for three days, but she still found it tempting to sink back into blankness now. She closed her eyes and rested her head on the worn cushion. "Sleep's not a problem."

"Well, then tell me the problem, Bree." Sammy perched on the arm of the sofa, her pale brows furrowed. "You don't return my calls. You've been dodging me for months, almost since the wedding. Is it Matt or what? It was just you and me for too many years to pull this kind of crap now, don't you think?"

Brenna regarded her sister for a moment, contrition warring with weariness. "Sam, I'm crazy about Matt. I know I've been scarce…I *am* sorry, kid. It's just this new job. It's pretty demanding."

"How demanding could it be? You work a nine-hour shift at the Clinic. You put in three times that during your internship, and you still managed to catch a burger with me once a week." Sammy's voice gentled, and she nudged Brenna with her knee. "What do they have you doing down there that's taking so much out of you?"

"Sam, you know I can't tell you about Clinic studies. It's Government work. I signed a confidentiality—"

"Yeah, Bree, I know," Samantha cut in, sliding down onto the cushion beside her. "But I also know that being a medic is the first thing in your entire life that's made you happy. You, like, *glowed* every day of that internship! I glowed too. I was so glad you had someone else to practice CPR on, finally."

"And minor surgery, and setting fractures." Brenna touched her sister's knee. "You remember me slathering you with red fingernail polish?"

"So you could practice trauma medicine." A reluctant smile curved Sammy's full lips. "And you stole the paddleboard the Ghoul whomped us all with, to use as a splint. I thought she was gonna kill us both."

"She wanted to."

"You didn't let her though." The love in Sammy's voice was tender and rich. "You told her if she laid one porky finger on me, you'd report her sneaking her scuzzy boyfriend into the girls' dorm at night. You kept them all off me, Bree. For years."

"Well." Brenna lifted her little sister's hand into her lap and played with her fingers. "Medicine's not the first thing in my life that made me happy, Sam."

"Well then, *talk* to me!" Samantha gripped her hand. "There's never been anything we couldn't talk about, Bree. Tell me what's going on at that Clinic that has you downing a fifth of Scotch every—"

"Sammy, not again. Okay?" Brenna pushed herself out of the sunken couch and went to the kitchen. "If it eases your mind, I haven't had a drink in days. You want coffee?"

"Yours?" Samantha shuddered. "Look, don't yell, but we've never run a genetic trace on our parents. We have no idea how deep problems with booze might run in our family. I just don't want to see you turn into one of those people who smuggle gin to work in a thermos someday."

"Samantha!" Brenna lowered her voice. "Listen. You were right to worry about the liquor, okay? I agree with that. I was hitting it way too heavy. But I can't drink now. My head needs to stay clear. Honest, Sammy. If I can't stay away from it now, I'll worry about me, too."

Samantha's face darkened. "Bree, what kind of trouble are you in?"

"I'm fine." Brenna didn't hesitate. "I'm just a little crazy trying to adjust to this new unit. Give me some time, honey. Please don't worry."

Samantha studied her silently for several seconds. "Okay. I'll trust you. I'll try not to worry. If you'll try to pick up your fucking phone once in a blue moon."

"Deal." Brenna smiled wearily. "Hey. Did you want me to look at that day-care permit? Did you bring the application?"

"I didn't come about the application." Sammy got up and lifted her keys from the side table. "I can't be late to work. I need a glowing reference from my boss if we want day care, period, City-sponsored or not."

"You've never had less. Give Matt my love." Brenna swallowed. "Thanks for coming, kid."

Samantha smiled, but her eyes were still troubled. She went to the door. "I hope you decide to talk to me soon about whatever the hell is eating you, Bree. You've never shut me out before. I just don't think sisters should treat each other like this."

The screen door latched quietly behind her. Brenna waited until the rumbling of Samantha's decrepit coupe receded down the street, and then she sank back down on the sofa. She wouldn't hear her sister's voice again for a very long time, but her last words would stay with her.

The liquor had backfired on Brenna four nights ago. Her dreams were cacophonous nightmares of drumming hooves, dying stallions, and crumbling cliffs. Sobriety didn't keep the dreams entirely at bay, but if she didn't drink, she could usually wake herself up before the spear was cast.

She stared through her tangled bangs at the dust motes dancing in a narrow beam of sunlight on the carpet. Jess was right. She did have choices. She could try to talk Caster out of terminating her placement for allowing a patient inappropriate contact. That seemed unlikely. Or she could resign voluntarily.

She had circled these fates endlessly, like a frozen buzzard waiting for the clean surge of relief that would mark the decision made.

She couldn't stop what was happening to Jess. No entry-level medic had that power. The clinical trials would continue with or without Brenna. And without the little protection she might once have afforded her patient. Her role as a medical advocate had been compromised. She saw again Caster's leering eagerness in the doorway of the detention cell, studying her with interest as she stepped back out of Jess's arms...

There was a side to Brenna that was almost ruthless, and she needed it now. A healthy instinct for self-preservation had delivered her, and Samantha as well, through almost ten years of Government foster care.

She was slipping badly, and Caster knew it. It was time to cut her losses.

Brenna struggled out of the sofa. She could be in and out of the Clinic an hour before Caster's second trial began. There would be no need to see Jess again.

❖

Sunglasses hid the worst of the wreckage the past days had made of Brenna's face. She peered at her wan reflection in the bulletproof glass of the Clinic's front entrance, then slid her ID badge through the scanner. She glanced at the security camera over the door, waiting. Charlotte took her sweet tacky-bitch time buzzing her in.

Caster's secretary regarded Brenna narrowly from her immaculate desk, her lacquered nails tapping an ominous cadence. "Don't bother with the charts, Brenna. Caster is waiting. She's in the gymnasium."

"Thanks, Charlotte."

"Brenna? I said don't bother with the charts. The gymnasium is that way—"

"Staff lockers are this way."

Charlotte's droning protest faded behind Brenna as she moved through the antiseptic chill of the Military Research unit. She wanted to remove the silver flask from her locker and dispose of it before she met with Caster. When Government employees were terminated, they weren't allowed to clear out their belongings without a security escort. Brenna didn't want a charge of drinking on duty to shatter what was left of her career.

She turned a corner and all but collided with Dugan in the doorway of the staff lounge.

"Whoa, Miss Brenna!" Dugan kept his hands on her arms. She noted absently that his face still carried the bruises Jess gave him in the arena. "Missus Mad Scientist herself directed me to escort you to the gym, stat, if I ran into you. Or you into me."

"I know where we're setting up, Dugan. Thanks. I'll be there." Brenna tried to brush past, but the big man's grip on her arms tightened, turning her away from the lounge.

"Sorry, baby doc. You might get some charge out of bucking Caster, but this boy plans to keep his job, even after that little mountain village up there is vulture fodder."

Brenna let herself be walked back toward the reception area, numbed by the same odd detachment that got her off the sofa. She knew she should be at least faintly alarmed by this forceful summons, but time was her main focus now. She glanced at the wire-meshed clock high on the wall over Charlotte's desk as they passed it. Jess would be taken from her detention cell in less than an hour. The confrontation with Caster would have to be brief.

Then the most logical reason for Caster's urgency made it through Brenna's haze, and she wrested her elbow from Dugan's grip. "Has something happened to my patient?"

Dugan seemed startled by her sudden energy.

"Um, is there a problem?" Charlotte leaned far over her desk to watch them, obviously hoping so. "Should I call Security?"

"I *am* Security, Charlotte," Dugan barked. "I think I can handle one woman all by myself."

"That's what you thought in the arena, Dugan." Brenna spun and walked toward the gymnasium. Jess should have been allowed to rest and heal the past three days. Surely Caster would have paged her at home if anything had happened. Brenna didn't see the brick red flush of anger filling Dugan's face as he followed.

❖

Gymnasium was a misnomer. That was what Clinic staff called the echoing chamber that served as the facility's indoor arena. It was used in foul weather or for any clinical or chemical trials deemed too sensitive for the eyes of general staff. The Tristaine study had been reclassified.

Brenna muscled open the heavy steel doors, and she saw Jess at once.

She stood beside Caster in the center of the hardwood floor, arms folded, her eyes darkening as they locked on Brenna's. The open collar of her black shirt framed the ugly stunner burn at the base of her throat. Fading bruises on her tense arms were still apparent as well. But Jess was whole and on her feet. Brenna felt suddenly lightheaded with relief.

Jess felt sucker punched. The memory of the soft warmth of Brenna's lips filled her, as it had relentlessly, for days. She had prayed to the goddesses guiding Tristaine that Brenna would never set foot in the Clinic again, for her own sake. This couldn't end well for either of them.

"Thank you, Mr. Dugan." Caster's tailored white coat glowed in the overhead fluorescents. She had just slipped a blood pressure cuff off the prisoner's upper arm and was recording figures on her omnipresent clipboard. "Welcome back, dear. You're nice and prompt."

Brenna forced her focus away from Jess to her supervisor's smiling face. The friendliness of the greeting threw her. She registered the presence of Karney, cradling two rifles, and Stuart, watching her avidly from his stool next to the video camera. Behind her, Dugan closed the doors to the gym and locked them, and Karney tossed him one of the rifles.

"Caster, I'm not staying." Brenna's voice echoed in the cavernous space as she closed the distance separating her from the scientist. Caster kept her position beside the prisoner, so Jess would hear. Brenna couldn't help that. "I came in to file my resignation from Military Research. I've decided to leave the Clinic."

"I see." A line appeared between Caster's neatly plucked brows, and her lips pursed unhappily as she studied Brenna. She turned to the table beside her, opened a medical kit, and took out a small vial and a square of gauze. "Brenna, I honestly don't know what to say. Can you tell me why?"

Brenna couldn't look at Jess. "This project...isn't a good match for me."

"But you're so highly skilled!" Caster dabbed some of the liquid onto the gauze. "And you must know the Clinic is the crème de la crème of Federal research facilities."

"I've lost my taste for Government work." Brenna didn't know why Caster was doing this, but she couldn't prolong this discussion. The silent Amazon was taking up all the air in this massive room, and she had to get out of there. "My decision is final, Caster. I'll leave the forms on your desk."

Run like hell, Brenna, Jess thought.

"Really, dear. All this, just because you allowed your patient to seduce you?"

Brenna stopped.

Dugan hooted softly and nudged Karney, who looked away.

"I suppose it does complicate things, dear, but perhaps it's all for the best." Caster poured more liquid onto the gauze pad. "If Jesstin is truly drawn to you, as opposed to simply using you, we can exploit that. You're all the more valuable to us because

Jesstin will be especially impacted by any punishment you administer. It might make an interesting sidebar to our journal article someday."

"You don't understand," Brenna said tonelessly. "I'm out of here. I didn't become a medic to…Caster, I'm not coming back."

"I'm sorry, Brenna, but I can't allow that." Caster regarded her seriously. "It's very important to me that this project succeed, dear. It could form the cornerstone of my career. Of all our careers. Losing a medical technician at this stage would be disastrous, at least on paper. Something like that might even be enough to hurt our funding."

Brenna felt sweat bead on her forehead. "You don't listen very well, lady. I've had it with this place and with you." She turned and started toward the doors to the gym.

Caster's voice rang sweetly to the steel rafters. "Do you have any idea how long you'll spend in Prison, Brenna? For stealing narcotics from the Clinic dispensary?"

Brenna turned and stared at her.

Jess's concern for Brenna cranked up another notch. She doubted Brenna had ever encountered Caster's blend of genteel amorality and ambition. She could only hope she had the sense to fear it.

"I asked Mr. Dugan here to break into your locker yesterday, Brenna. He slipped about five thousand dollars' worth of morphia capsules in there. I reported them missing from the dispensary this morning. There's a shiny new lock on your locker now, and I have the only key."

Brenna's hands filled with a tingling numbness.

"Sweet little flask, dear. A gift from your sister?"

"This girl's no threat to you, Caster." Jess's voice was filled with gravel. She hadn't spoken in three days. "Leave her alone."

Brenna saw Dugan shift the rifle in his arms. Caster turned to Jess with arched brows.

"Oh, come, Jesstin." Caster moved closer to her and patted

the soaked gauze tenderly over the stunner burn at the base of her throat. "You can't hope to distract me from the fate of this pretty little slattern by so overtly drawing my fire."

Jess stiffened and closed her eyes. Brenna realized the solution Caster was using on the burn was tecathenase, or something equally caustic.

Caster turned to Brenna with the patient air of one summing up the obvious. "Sexual contact with a prisoner is grounds for dismissal, Brenna. That, and drinking on the job, will ensure that you never work in a medical setting again, not in this City. But you may not require employment, because you could be sitting next door in our cozy Prison, for ten to fifteen years." She smiled. "Jesstin, tell us how long petite young blondes last among violent inverts—"

Jess's hand shot out and caught Caster's slender wrist. "You sick City harpy—"

"Jesstin, don't!" Brenna cried.

Caster shrieked and Dugan bellowed. Karney was closer to Jess and reached her first, jamming the end of his rifle into her neck. Dugan wrenched her arms behind her. Stuart rose from his stool but quickly sat back down. He had watched the tape of the Amazon in the arena three times.

Jess thought for a moment Karney would fire, out of sheer rattled nerves. She allowed Caster to yank her arm free.

Caster's jeweled wristwatch fell with a glassy clatter to the hardwood floor. "Dugan," she gasped, holding her wrist tightly between her white-coated breasts. "Get this fucking savage away from me!" She whirled on Brenna, a strand of her silver hair dangling over one cheek. "Make your decision, girl. Prison, or your worthless name on a prestigious Government study?"

Brenna closed her eyes for a moment, but she had no gods to pray to. She walked toward Jess, not hearing the hollow echo of her steps on the floor. She looked up at Dugan. "Let go of her."

Amused, Dugan backed off, raising a hand in mock obedience.

Karney lowered his rifle. "Brenna, this sucks." He glanced at Caster, his voice low. "But I have a family."

Brenna didn't hear him either. She spoke to Jess quietly. "I don't have a choice in this."

"There are always choices."

"I can't go to Prison."

"Then that's your choice, Bren."

"Remove the prisoner's shirt, please, Brenna." Caster was recovering her poise.

Brenna's hands were steady as she tugged the snaps of Jess's black shirt apart, then reached up to slide it down her arms. She folded it neatly.

"Let's begin." Caster patted her silver hair in place. "Jesstin, I've devised a protocol for our second trial that fairly reeks with Amazonian authenticity. Mr. Dugan, Mr. Karney? Please bind our subject between those two uprights there at the far wall. Stuart, go with them and set up the camera."

She bent beneath the table and withdrew a coiled whip, shining and rough as a black rawhide snake. "Brenna, you're to flog Jesstin until she either passes out or agrees to sign the renunciation. Be careful now. It took me months to master this thing. It's tricky. You'd best take a few practice strikes before we roll tape."

Brenna watched Jess walk toward the far wall of the gym. Dugan and Karney kept their distance on either side of her. She felt Caster's arm slide gently across her shoulders, and her throat filled with a burning thirst for vodka.

"I know this will be difficult for you, dear. But try to keep in mind that our ultimate goal is the salvation of Jesstin's mountain village. If we're able to make the women of Tristaine law-abiding Government citizens, we'll actually save their lives! Without us, they'll die in a bloody, explosive war they have no hope of winning."

Brenna watched as the two men leaned their rifles against the far wall, then took Jess's arms and stretched them between the two standing poles. Her bare back gleamed under the gymnasium's harsh light. Dugan said something to Karney and laughed. Karney just fumbled with the cuffs, trying to find the release.

"And if we can break Jesstin's spirit before we break her body," Caster continued, "then she'll live too. There could be no greater justification for your participation in this study, yes?"

She offered Brenna the bullwhip. Brenna looked at it dully, then reached for the leather grip.

"Hey!"

"Fuck, Kar—"

Jess took Karney out neatly with a spinning kick to the crotch, then Dugan with a heel to the kidneys. Stuart promptly dropped both chair and camera with a crash and bolted toward the alarm lever on the opposite wall. Jess let him go.

She targeted the two women across the length of the long gymnasium and ran.

Caster screamed in genuine terror. She jerked Brenna around in front of her to use her body as a shield. She fumbled with the stunner in her coat pocket, then saw the insanity in the sprinting prisoner's face, and she froze. The stunner was a toy in the face of such rage.

She heaved Brenna forward, a sacrificial offering to slow the demon down, and bolted for the back door. She almost fell, looking back to see how far the rabid Amazon had to run before she was disemboweled by her teeth. She staggered to a halt, astonished. The madwoman wasn't coming after her. She was targeted on the insipid young medic!

Jess vaulted to the table and used it to launch a soaring dive. At that moment the air split apart as Stuart yanked on the alarm lever, filling the gym with a screaming siren.

Brenna waited, watching Jess's blazing fury descend toward her. She felt both fear and relief. She could have run, but she didn't.

"Bloody traitor!" Jess screamed.

Her body crashed into Brenna and carried them both to

the floor. Brenna fell hard and then slid a good three yards on the polished wood, Jess's weight crushing the air from her lungs. She heard the siren, the yells of the men, Caster's strident commands. Strong hands encircled her throat.

Jess snarled loudly, then bent over Brenna and pressed her lips to her ear. "I'm choking you. Fight me. Listen. This won't save you, Brenna. She's got you now."

Jess raised her head, filled her lungs, and emitted a blood-chilling howl. Her arms locked, shaking, but her grip around Brenna's throat remained loose and relaxed.

"Dugan, Karney, no!" Caster sounded frantic as she snatched up the bullwhip. "You can't shoot her from there, you cretins. You might kill her! Run, run!"

"Listen to me," Jess spat. "Get out of here, Brenna, out of the City. She has her hooks in you, and she'll never let go."

Brenna finally pulled breath back into her lungs. She heard thunderclapping footsteps and saw Caster loom above them. They were out of time.

"Leave her!" Caster shouted at Dugan as he and Karney reached them. She snapped out the bullwhip. "This protocol will be followed, Jesstin, one way or another."

"There are always choices," Jesstin whispered to Brenna, and then Caster's whip cracked across her bare back like a gunshot. She gasped raggedly.

"Caster!" Brenna was frozen, half-pinned under Jess's long body as the lash descended again. The oiled tip of the bullwhip struck Jess's upper shoulder, inches from Brenna's eyes.

"Get out of there, Brenna," Caster snapped. "Assist her, Mr. Dugan! Jesstin, are you quite sure you don't want to put a stop to this?"

Jess made no reply, and Brenna twisted out from under her. She didn't think. She just sprawled across her patient to shield her. Caster couldn't stop the lash's trajectory in time, and it snapped hard across Brenna's stomach. She felt the strike through her shirt, and she almost fainted.

"Idiot," Jess panted. It was all she had breath for.

Dugan grabbed Brenna roughly and hauled her to her feet, and Caster resumed the beating.

Jess stayed down, braced by her forearms on the gymnasium floor. She shuddered under the repeated cracks of the whip across her back, but she didn't cry out. Brenna's gesture made Amazon macha important again, somehow. She felt blood trickle from one of the welts, wending down to her waist, but she remained silent.

Brenna forced herself to stand still between Dugan and Karney and watch the scourging numbly. She could almost feel the color drain from her face. Her eyes remained tearless and fixed.

Finally Caster coiled the whip, her smooth face glistening. "My, that's quite a workout! I'm afraid my arm gave out before our stubborn subject did." She patted her wrist to her forehead. "It's unfortunate that your display of temper prevented proper filming of this trial, Jesstin. We'll have to come up with something truly cinematic for your next session. Mr. Karney, escort the prisoner back to her cell, please."

Brenna watched numbly as Karney pulled Jess to her feet. She was conscious, but only technically, and she couldn't stand without the burly orderly's support. Brenna looked up at Dugan silently until he released her with a mocking grin. Then she addressed Caster. "You have to let me treat her back."

"Certainly, dear, if you're willing. She's quite subdued now." A pretty flush of exertion tinged Caster's cheeks, and she smoothed her silver cloud of hair carefully. "Use the tecathenase."

"Caster." Brenna discovered she was willing to beg.

"Tecathenase or nothing," Caster said firmly. "And we won't be able to give Jesstin as much recovery time from now on, Brenna. Her clinicals continue tomorrow. I'm sorry, dear, but that's what the whittling process is all about."

❖

Jess heard Brenna's voice first, which was fortunate. The rest of her awakening was distinctly less pleasant. She lay face down on the restrainer, which had been adjusted to lie flat. Her shirt was still off. Her back felt wrapped in sheets of flame.

The soothing voice above her fell silent, and she felt cold fingers on her arm.

"Can you tell me how bad it is, Jess?"

"How do you do that?" Jess mumbled.

"What?"

"Know when I'm awake." Jess opened her eyes in stages. "I just found out myself."

"Your body tenses up. Whoa, yeah, like that." Brenna put her arm across her hips as Jess's nerve endings awoke in full. "Yell if you need to, Jess. It's okay."

"I can't. Too macha." The nausea receded, and Jess craned her neck to see Brenna. "You all right?"

"I'm fine." Brenna smiled wanly, because she knew how *fine* she looked. "I'm going to finish washing your back. It's just water. It's all I can do, but it's better than nothing. I'm not putting that tecathenase acid on this."

Jess rested her chin on her crossed hands. She could feel the warmth from the arc lamp on her flayed shoulders, and she tried to quell the fine trembling in her gut. "How much time do I have?"

Brenna shook back the white sleeve of her lab coat and checked her watch. "It's evening. Maybe fourteen hours." The strain was back in her voice. "You can't take another session like this tomorrow, Jess. I doubt if you'll be able to walk by then."

"I'll walk." Jess closed her eyes.

Brenna paused. "That stunt you pulled, jumping me like that."

"Didn't work, did it?" Jess sighed. "If Caster let you in here alone with me, she doesn't believe I'm going to tear out your aorta. I wanted to stop her from using you against me."

"I know. But you did it for me, too, didn't you? So I wouldn't have to…"

"Not all for you, Bren. Caster's right. It would have been worse for me if you'd held the whip."

Brenna stared at her. She continued sponging her back, and for a while there was only the sound of water being rinsed from the cloth.

Jess felt tears rising and made no effort to stop them.

"Jesstin?"

Jess scrubbed her face on her forearm. "Just homesick."

Brenna rinsed the cloth in the basin again and watched the water swirl with red. "You were out of it for a while, Jess. You said a few things. Names. Like Kyla, and Shann, some others I didn't catch."

It didn't matter, Jess told herself. The Military had had files on Shann for years. She hadn't revealed anything vital. But if she was spouting off like that in her sleep, then she was losing control, and that worried her.

"Was anyone else around?" Jess's breath caught as the new tension in her shoulders started an unfortunate chain reaction, locking her muscles again.

"No, we were alone. Will you settle down, please?" When Jess was able to relax again on the chair's padded surface, Brenna rested her hand on the thick hair at the base of her neck. "Jess, just lie there for a second. Don't go on until you feel better."

Jess complied. Her breathing steadied. "I feel better," she mumbled.

Brenna laid the wet cloth against a welt high on her shoulder. "Camryn and Kyla, they're your friends in the Prison. Right? And they're both like you, they're Amazons?"

"We're from Tristaine." Jess's brogue was subdued. "Long story. 'Amazons' will do. We use the word ourselves. Cam and Ky were arrested soon after I was. For trying to spring me, as Camryn put it. The little saps."

"Spring you?"

"Well, they're Amazons."

"Spring you from a Federal lockup?"

"They're adolescent Amazons." Jess made the effort to smile. "And they came pretty close to pulling it off." She tightened for a moment, as Brenna patted the cloth across her raw shoulder blade.

"Kyla and Camryn." Brenna repeated the names. "They knew your friend Dyan, too? And the girl who was with her, Laurel?"

"Lauren," Jess corrected. "Lauren was Camryn's younger sister, by blood. Dyan was Kyla's older one."

Brenna exhaled sharply. "Lord, Jess."

"They're my adanin, so they came after me. They should have waited for Shann." She closed her eyes. "This hurts like a bitch, Bren."

"I know it does. Stay with me. You're doing great."

Jess's back and shoulders were striped with lash marks of no discernible pattern. The whip had cut deeply enough into her tanned skin to draw blood several times. Brenna felt again the shocking, fiery sting of the single stroke she'd taken. She tried to multiply that by thirty.

Her fingers tightened on the cloth. Inexorably but gently, she kept it moving. Her other hand still rested in Jess's hair, scratching her head lightly. "I don't know why you're not screaming. Anyone else would be."

"What are you going to do about Caster, Brenna?"

Brenna stilled her fingers. "Don't worry about that now. I can take care of myself."

"You haven't done very well so far."

"Pardon me, here." She slid her fingers out of Jess's hair. "I got by for twenty-three years before either you or Caster showed up. And my life hasn't been the fun little potluck you seem to think it has." She made sure none of her annoyance showed in her hands. Her touch on Jess's back remained light and careful.

"I don't doubt that, lass. I'm sitting up."

"No, you're not. Jesstin, damn it!"

Brenna argued while Jess pushed herself up on her arms, then shifted, very carefully, until her legs dangled over the side of the recliner. She rested her hands on the leather surface, sat up straight, and took a deep breath, waiting for the cell to settle again. She looked at Brenna. "Have you been crying?"

Brenna's professional appearance had been partially restored by the white lab coat, but she was almost as pale as Jess felt, and her eyes were bleak with recent tears. "I do this all the time. It's just nerves." Brenna scrubbed the back of one hand across her face. "Am I going to have to tie you down to get you to hold still?"

"I won't obey you anymore, Bren."

Brenna blinked.

Jess let that news flash sink in. "Do you believe me, about the murders?"

A dozen replies occurred to Brenna, but when her mouth opened, only the truth emerged. "I don't know what to believe, anymore."

Jess accepted that. Twenty years under this regime was a heavy load to shake off in one week. "I hope you're as strong as I think you are." She lifted her chin toward the door. "You need to get home."

"What?"

"You should have left at least an hour ago. You're being blackmailed. It's best to keep up appearances until you know what to do. Right?"

"Right." Brenna walked around the restrainer and tossed the folded cloth in the sink. "Listen. Two things." She rested her hand on the porcelain and turned to Jess. "I've decided…I do want to help you, if I can. I feel some responsibility in this. But I've got to protect myself, too, Jesstin. To do that, I have to at least pretend to cooperate with Caster."

"Agreed." Jess leaned forward and rested her elbows gingerly on her knees. "Second?"

"Second." Brenna's throat moved as she swallowed. "I don't want you to touch me again, without my permission."

The light in Jess's eyes dimmed. "All right, Bren."

Brenna looked at her. Jess's face glistened with sweat, and she was trembling. Then Jess smiled at her reassuringly, and Brenna felt tears threaten again.

"Go home," Jess said gently. "And don't drink, Brenna."

She said nothing for a moment, then went back to the restrainer. "Will you be able to sleep?"

"Sure." Jess made a deliberate effort to relax her shoulders.

"Lie down first, please." Brenna smiled crookedly. "That's not an order, but it's sound medical advice." Her hand hovered above Jess's forearm. "Try to rest, Jesstin."

"You too."

Brenna clicked off the overhead light and felt her way to the door of the cell. Then she went through it and locked the prisoner in for the night.

CHAPTER FIVE

The cold of the cell's cement floor bled through Jess's black linen trousers. She sat with her long legs crossed, braced against the cinder block. She rested her back against the wall briefly, then winced and lifted it. The meager breakfast tray had come and gone an hour ago. They would come for her soon.

She had prayed, on and off, since dawn. Or as best as she could gauge sunrise behind stone walls. Cold concrete was a poor substitute for the mountain meadows Jess preferred for prayer, but the floor was better than the restraining chair. Its padded length might be more comfortable, but she couldn't speak to her goddesses on a device used to confine her.

Jess figured Gaia wasn't particular about posture anyway. She'd never seen Shann kneel when she prayed. Shann tended to wave her arms around and yell a lot when she communed with her Mothers, stalking up and down the rows of Tristaine's gardens, her preferred chapel. Jess had always taken a similar conversational approach with her own deities.

This young woman was raised in the bleak void of the City, she reminded them. *Please, my Mothers, give her the courage to escape these spiritual butchers with her soul intact. She touches me...don't let me be the reason she loses her way. And your daughters, Camryn and Kyla. Keep them safe too. If you ask me, you owe Tristaine. For Dyan and for Lauren. Cherish your children now.*

Jess heard the electronic hum that released the lock of her cell door, and she battled a brief wave of dizziness as she got to her feet. She closed her eyes again for a last petition.

Guide us home by your path, and make us strong.

❖

"Stuart, roll film!"

Jess was blinded at first by the stage lighting Stuart had erected to shine on the entrance to the gymnasium. She walked into a silver glare and immediately loosened her body until her eyes adjusted. Anything could fly straight at her and she wouldn't see it. She had to be ready to move.

Her vision cleared soon enough. Though Stuart's camera was pointed toward Jess, fully half of the echoing gym had been brightened by floodlights. She saw Caster regarding her from a far wall, smiling, her hands folded over her clipboard. Her slender wrist bore a shiny new watch. She stood next to the two upright posts.

Brenna stood between them, her spread arms cuffed high enough to stretch her to full height. She was naked to the waist. Fear emanated from her in waves, but her voice was clear and sharp.

"Don't move, Jesstin. You stay there. Are you listening to me?"

"Keep filming, Stuart," Caster urged. She watched Jess with bright interest.

Jess walked past Dugan, the only Clinic staff in the gymnasium besides Stuart and Caster, as if his rifle didn't exist. Part of her registered that Karney was not present. Perhaps he felt Caster's bonus wasn't sweet enough to cover this.

After that first sickening blast of adrenaline, Jess was calm, and her body reflected it. She stopped when Caster indicated, by clearing her throat, that she'd come as close to Brenna as would be allowed.

"Caster." Brenna spoke without deference or pleading. "Let me talk to her. Privately."

Caster pursed her lips, looking from Jess to Brenna. She

did toss a quick glance at Dugan to make sure the big orderly and his rifle were close, then returned to savoring her reply to Brenna's request.

"I don't think so, Brenna. Not right now. All Jesstin needs to hear, at this juncture, is that your participation in today's protocol is not entirely coerced."

Jess was careful to show no reaction, but her stomach clenched. She stood twenty feet from the bound woman, studied her eyes, and knew Caster was telling the truth. Brenna had agreed to this.

"Why?" she asked her.

The merciless light on her exposed breasts was an inescapable horror, but Brenna's voice was level. "All right. I'm thinking two things. First, you can't take any more of this, Jess. You've had enough. You've been beaten for weeks."

"Second?"

"Stuart? You can cut for now." Caster strolled in front of Brenna, flicking another glance at Dugan's rifle for reassurance. "Please, ladies, there's no need to string this out. Allow me to summarize."

Caster nodded. "Brenna and I struck a deal this morning, Jesstin, before you joined us. Brenna has agreed to participate in today's new protocol. And after today, she walks. She'll be allowed to resign. She can limp off quietly and work in some destitute ghetto infirmary somewhere, with my blessings. Are you following so far?"

As far as Jess was concerned, she and Brenna were alone in the gym. "Tell me your second thought, Bren."

"Second." Brenna's hands gripped the narrow chains binding them to the posts. "Second is, I'm not willing to go to Prison. But I'm not willing to hurt you any more either, Jess. I'm a medic. I…that's all I ever wanted to be."

Now Brenna did plead and she saw Jess's gaze soften. "So just do it. Whatever you have to do, whatever she says. If we can get through this, she'll let me resign, and you won't be hurt again.

I made her promise that. Jesstin, a few days of pain are worth it to me."

She searched Jess's face, the tension in her arms matching the strain on her frayed nerves. A shield had dropped across Jess's features. She couldn't read her now.

"I'm supposed to whip you, then?" Jess asked Brenna, pleasantly.

"That's right," Caster confirmed. "Jesstin, I'm going to move to the table over there, to get you your whip. Please mind Mr. Dugan's rifle, yes?"

Jess stood still as Caster stepped gingerly past her. Her thought process was poleaxed. She prayed it would cough up a clue soon, and hoped her relaxed facade was convincing, because she was stumped. She had no idea what to do.

Caster retrieved the bullwhip from the box beneath the table. "You Amazons are probably adept with these things. Jesstin, would you join me, please?" She caressed the coils of the whip affectionately. "This tape will probably be the one featured in the documentary, so look lively, please."

Dugan trained his scope briefly on the swell of Brenna's left thigh. He squinted to the side to check Jess as she moved toward the table, then focused on the cuffed blonde again. He could do it, he decided. He could pull the trigger. On either of them.

Caster waited until Jess reached her, then handed her the bullwhip. Then she bent beneath the table again and pulled out a cylinder the size of a cheap flashlight. She switched it on, and the device engaged with a muted buzzing sound.

She looked up at Stuart. "Good morning, ladies and gentlemen." Her clarion tones rang sweetly through the gym.

"This date marks the opening of the second clinical trial of Study T-714, already referenced in the previous clip. Please consult my addendum to our prospectus, faxed to each of you this date. As I summarized therein, we have already established in our first trial that our subject, Jesstin of Tristaine, will not capitulate under sustained physical duress."

Jess studied the coiled whip in her hands, then studied Brenna through the glaring light. She stood quietly between the uprights with her head lowered, but she wasn't trembling now. Jess noticed Brenna's breathing, its deliberate pace and slow rhythm. She followed her example and began to prepare herself.

"Several days ago, I instructed my associate, our study's medical advocate, to initiate a sexual relationship with our subject, here." Caster smiled, as if to accommodate the expected gasps of her audience. "All right, true. Unconventional means! But that's why you contracted with the Clinic, yes? For the creative, cutting edge only we can bring to Military research?"

She nodded at Stuart, who panned back to include Brenna, suspended between the two posts, in his viewfinder. Stuart focused carefully. He wasn't looking forward to this trial, but he could still enjoy the image in the frame. He had long nursed a massive crush on Caster's assistant.

Caster paused again, politely, to allow any renewed furor in her audience to subside. "I'll not be so crass as to tell you this is your tax dollars at work, ladies and gentlemen, but please, don't be concerned. Brenna is fully compliant with our protocol and is being well compensated for her participation."

She gestured to Jess with the crackling cylinder. "Jesstin here has developed quite an interpersonal bond with young Brenna. And today, as per my addendum, she will be required to inflict rather severe physical pain on the woman she loves, until she agrees to renounce Tristaine."

"Caster." Jess ignored the camera, and she'd grown accustomed to the stage lighting. She spoke to the other woman intimately, with genuine curiosity. "You know I'll refuse."

The smile remained on Caster's unlined face. "Well, Jesstin. If you refuse to flog Brenna, I'm afraid I'll have to ask Mr. Dugan here to trade his rifle for this little toy." She lifted the buzzing cylinder. "And use it on your amorata, yonder, as he sees fit. It carries rather more of a wallop than our staff's tame stunners."

Jess eyed the device dispassionately.

Caster switched off the electric prod with a smart click. "Both you and poor Brenna can avoid all this unpleasantness, of course, if you'll sign this document now."

She turned toward Stuart and showed her clipboard to the camera. "A simple statement, ladies and gentlemen. Jesstin's signature will affirm that she will pay our fair City taxes. Obey City laws. And, in return, receive the bounty of the City's amenities, as one of its citizens."

Brenna strained to hear her response. Caster's camera-ready words reached her clearly, but she still had no clue as to what Jess was thinking. The white static of fear kept filling her mind.

Jess nodded, slowly studying the document. "And what will you do with it? This statement."

"It's the act of signing itself that's the point of the trial, Jesstin." Caster lowered the clipboard, eager to move on. "It's symbolic. Now, if you've reached a decision—"

"Yeah, I understand that," Jess interrupted. "But your goal is to incorporate all of Tristaine, right? Not just recruit me." She lifted her chin at Dugan. "Is your poodle over there going to fly a helicopter over my village and drop copies of my surrender? Something like that?"

"Amazon bitch." Dugan pointed his rifle toward Jess's heart, then lowered it in frustration. The rifle was partly a bluff, and the prisoner knew it. He would lose his job if he killed her. Caster had instructed him to aim for the legs, and then only if she attacked staff again.

"Be very careful, Jesstin." Caster spoke quietly, but the sides of her nostrils flared white. "I would be fully justified in applying this prod to your belly right now."

Jess thought about it. "I have to speak to Brenna before I do this."

Caster narrowed her eyes. She balanced her desire to proceed with the sheer havoc this big hoodlum could create if this simple request was denied. "Very well, Jesstin. Quickly, please."

For a moment, Brenna was dazzled by the sheer theatricality of the backlit image moving across the gym toward her. Jess stopped immediately in front of her, her face shielded with the shadow created by her wide shoulders.

Jess's voice was low. "Are you all right, Bren?"

"I will be." Brenna's teeth were chattering. "Jesstin, what are you doing?"

"Don't talk, please. Listen to me. Brenna, she's lying to you. This won't end until Tristaine is taken. You have to get out of the City."

"Jess, you just heard—"

"Shut up," Jess said quietly. "You'll bleed for nothing. She won't let you resign. This isn't your fight, Brenna. I can't let you do this."

Brenna started to speak, and Jess lifted a subtle hand to silence her. "Just make me one promise. I have friends on the inside. They'll come to you. Help them get Kyla and Camryn out. I'm counting on you, Bren."

"Who do you think you are, a bloody burning bush?" Nameless panic sluiced through Brenna. "Don't just spit out orders at me without—Jesstin! Jess!"

Brenna clenched her teeth. If she hissed any louder, Caster would hear her, and Jess didn't stop. Her relaxed stride carried her back to the table, the whip coiled easily in one hand.

Jess focused on Caster's face as it emerged through the glare of the flood lamps. Out of the corner of her eye, she saw the hooded lens of the camera swing slowly, following her progress. She noted Dugan had targeted the big muscle in her right calf.

"General Lorber, Dr. Aldin, Madam Undersecretary, I think we're ready to begin." Caster straightened, imagining the music the public documentarians would use to underscore this delicious tension. She held the electric prod where Jess could see it.

"Jesstin, you have endured weeks of physical punishment."

Caster was careful to sound somewhat compassionate. "And if my hypothesis is correct, you face even greater anguish today, if you choose to use this whip on one of your...adanin. Will you put an end to this now and sign the statement? Or will you administer the first ten lashes?"

Not without relish, Jess raised her hand and shot a stinging slap across Caster's scented cheek. Caster gasped harshly and would have fallen, but Jess hauled her upright and used her to block Dugan's rifle.

Dugan cursed and fired a round into the gym's rafters. The bullet's progress echoed crazily among the steel beams.

"Change in protocol." Jess smiled into Caster's white face.

Caster cried out as the silver rod was twisted inexorably out of her grasp. Jess turned the prod into the open collar of her own shirt and pressed it to her chest.

"Your granddaughters will mock your grave, Caster."

"Jesstin," Brenna screamed.

Jess flicked the rod's switch. She wouldn't let go of it, and Caster wasn't strong enough to break her grip, so the current shot through Jess's heart muscle in successive bursts.

Caster screamed for Dugan, who sent one of the floodlights crashing as he launched himself at Jess. He had his rifle twisted through her arms in seconds, and the sparking prod fell with a plank-denting clatter to the floor. Jess fell more slowly.

Brenna went witless with shock as she saw Jess's knees buckle. The broken hood of the floodlight rocked crazily, sending twisted shadows over the cavernous room. Her mind had switched to surreal, and the eerie light show made the scene before Brenna even less credible until she heard the flat crack of Jess's head hitting the hardwood floor.

Caster regained her composure and barked out orders like Uzi fire. "Stuart, camera off! This tape goes nowhere but in my safe! *Stuart!* Got that? Dugan, get Brenna down. I need her! Stuart, get a crash cart. Stat, stat!"

Caster knelt beside the motionless prisoner and heaved her onto her back. Jess's body turned bonelessly. Caster tore her black shirt open. The deep burn covering Jess's upper chest was ugly, but her utter stillness frightened Brenna far more.

"Dugan?" Brenna's mind mercifully switched channels again, searching the band until it found medic. She watched the big orderly run toward her, his keys jangling, his face brick red. "Dugan, you get here now. Get me out of these. Right now, Dugan." Her voice was perfectly calm.

"No respiration, no pulse," Caster called. She opened Jess's mouth and bent over her.

"It's that key. No, Dugan, the one you just tried. Hurry."

Brenna forced herself to stand still until both of her hands were released from the cuffs. She couldn't help her patient with a broken wrist. Then she ran, shaking her hands hard to restore circulation.

Caster finished the series of rescue breaths just as Brenna reached Jess and levered one leg over her waist to straddle her. She positioned her numb hands on her chest, locked her wrists, and began cardiac compressions, numbering them aloud automatically.

Brenna had narrowed most of her focus to carrying out this single, lifesaving function, and she worked efficiently, rocking with the compressions, not shedding a tear. The small part of her mind not thus occupied was filling again with static. Brenna was terrified.

"She can't do this to us." Caster bent for another round of rescue breaths. She looked haggard, and strands of silver hair wisped around her head as she blew into Jess's mouth, then straightened again.

Brenna sat back on Jess's waist, panting, staring at her unresponsive face. "Jess, come on now." Her voice was almost conversational, then it rose.

"Do you hear me? Jess? Open your eyes, Jesstin!" She pounded the reddened valley between Jess's breasts with her fist.

Jess's dark eyelashes fluttered against her pale cheek, and then her long body convulsed. She came to with a heaving gasp, and Brenna lunged across her to keep her flat.

Caster hovered, as if not willing to believe her good luck. Then she pulled herself to her feet and shook off Dugan's assistance. "Dugan, take this Amazon bitch and her half-naked little puta and toss them in a dark closet somewhere! I don't want to look at them again today! Brenna, you'd best talk this freakish invert out of her cretinous death wish by tomorrow morning!"

Caster spun on her heel and stalked toward the gymnasium doors. "Be convincing, young lady. Remember how easily I can still arrange your incarceration in adjoining cells on a more lasting basis."

❖

Jess remained conscious, but disturbingly passive. Dugan carried her out of the gym, and her stillness in the big orderly's arms told Brenna how dangerously weak she was.

Dugan took Caster's orders literally. He didn't let Brenna retrieve her shirt, and he didn't return them to the detention cell. He found a large, empty storeroom in B-wing instead and set Jess down, none too gently, on the concrete floor. Brenna went to her immediately.

"Hey, Miss Brenna." Dugan paused in the doorway, backlit by the light from the corridor, jiggling keys in his pocket. "You want me to call someone for you? Wait, you live alone. That's in your file, along with you being inverted. I got keys to every filing cabinet in the joint."

Brenna measured Jess's pulse at the throat. Still thready, but stronger than it had been in the gym.

Dugan sighed and kicked the doorjamb. "Hey, Brenna, I'm sorry about all this shit. But I've got to tell you, if you'd been a little more friendly around here, less stuck up, maybe you'd have more buddies now when you need 'em. You're in deep shit, girl."

Brenna didn't respond.

"Better you than me, I guess." Dugan shrugged. "You two sleep tight now. And don't let that Amazon do anything you wouldn't let me do. Which Caster will probably let me do to both of you eventually anyway. Night." He locked the storeroom door securely behind him, leaving them in darkness.

Brenna could see nothing until her eyes adjusted. The only light came from a shuttered window high on the opposite wall. She lifted Jess's head carefully into her lap, then leaned back against the swirled plaster wall, cringing a little at its cold roughness on her bare shoulders. She let out a shaking breath.

Her hand remained lightly on Jess's chest to monitor the even rise and fall of her breathing. Brenna closed her eyes, her fingers sifting through Jess's hair in instinctive comfort. She seemed to be sleeping rather than comatose, her respiration slow and deep.

I'll never sleep again, Brenna decided. It was the only concrete resolution she could make at the moment. Sleep was a waste of time, and she desperately needed time to think.

They had a brief respite. The Clinic's swing shift was just coming on. They had several hours before they would be returned to the gymnasium. *Before we will be returned.* Brenna tasted the word in her mouth. She and Jess had become "we."

Having time to think was no guarantee of clarity. Brenna's thoughts were too snarled in shock and dread and the warmth of the injured prisoner in her lap. She pictured the flask in her locker.

The trials would begin again in the morning. With the same protocol, or one very like it. Jess moaned softly in her sleep. Brenna bent over her, hesitated, then rested her lips briefly on her forehead.

The strange woman she held would never hurt her. Brenna knew that in her gut. Jess might even risk death again before allowing anyone else to harm her. Who was she to this Amazon? What could she have possibly done to merit that sacrifice?

Caster won't let you go. Brenna heard the certainty in Jess's voice again and shivered. She couldn't go to her sister for help. Samantha and Matthew lived in another part of the City, and Sammy was as protective of her as a bulldog. She couldn't endanger them. But Sam was the only person who would even feel her absence. She had no one else.

There were other Cities, in other Counties. But relocation required several permits, a financial audit, a medical screening, and multiple interviews with Immigration. It often took months, and Caster could derail that process at any stage if she wished. Brenna could just bolt, try to set up a false identity in another City, but that took money. She didn't have enough saved for phony ID, let alone the bribes that were probably necessary for illegal flight.

Flight.

❖

The magnificent horse gathered itself beneath her and glided over a yawning crevice in the rocky mountain path. It landed easily, and she with it, two creatures of blended spirit. Then the whickering sound of the spear, and the gut-punching cry of grief in her heart as the black stallion staggered and fell.

Brenna plummeted through empty space, screaming, twisting in helpless terror. Then she was brought up short with a jarring yank, caught by her wrists and ankles. She lifted her head, dazed, and found herself chained to a splintered wooden X-frame, her nude body spread beneath the brilliant flood lamps of the Clinic gymnasium. She pulled at her bonds in a nameless panic, but they held her fast.

A tall figure walked toward her, outlined by a nimbus of light, a whip coiled easily at her side. Brenna tossed her damp hair out of her eyes as Jess emerged from the glare, and her heated gaze held her riveted. She stopped inches from Brenna's suspended body, and her large hand rose and cupped her face. Brenna closed her eyes, savoring the rough touch of her palm.

She felt her nipples rise and harden, and her back arched slightly, offering her breasts, her breathing growing more rapid with her rising need. The coiled whip brushed lightly against the red-gold fur of her mound, and a soft moan escaped Brenna.

Jess slid the bunched leather across the flat planes of her belly. Her lips fastened on the taut skin of Brenna's throat, sucking gently, her warm breath sending cascading shudders through her bound limbs. The coiled whip tickled the lower swells of her breasts, then rasped against her aching nipples. Jess's head lowered, and her mouth fastened around one protruding bud. Her tongue swirled against it, and Brenna arched again, crying out softly.

The gymnasium dissolved around them, and in the way of dreams, Brenna found they were standing in the crystalline waters of a rushing river, the air around them fresh and sweet with birdsong. No longer chained, her hands found the tumbled wildness of Jess's hair and twined in it, moaning as her lips moved to Brenna's other breast and began a light, sucking caress.

Jess flinched, and Brenna awoke instantly. Her hand had brushed the burn at the base of her throat. She lifted it quickly, with a hiss of contrition.

"Have you been awake long?" Brenna straightened against the plaster wall, blinking hard to banish the fading disorientation of the dream. It was too dark to see anything but vague shapes. "How are you?"

"Is this a cell?" Jess muttered.

"We're in a storeroom. Are you in pain, Jess?"

"You should have let me go, Bren." Jess's soft brogue was hoarse.

"That's a bloody stupid thing to say. What were you thinking of, Jesstin? If Amazons really believe it's courageous to kill themselves every time they're under a little pressure, I understand why there are so few of you left! Is it…here, this is hurting your back. Turn on your side."

She helped Jess move to a less painful position and waited until her head settled on her thigh. When she spoke again, she softened her tone. "Does Amazon pride really mean so much to you that you'd throw away your life for it?"

"It's not that simple." Jess's eyes closed as Brenna's fingers drifted through her hair. "If my choices are betraying my family, torturing a friend, or escaping on my terms…" She sighed. "It's complicated, Bren."

"How do you feel?"

"Like I died and someone jumped up and down on my chest."

They rested in the cool, shadowed room.

Brenna felt oddly peaceful. Jess's hair warmed her belly, and the darkness made her near-nakedness easier to forget. As for Jess, resting on Brenna's muscular thigh seemed to lessen her pain.

"Caster was positive you'd sign the renunciation today." Brenna was exhausted. "If not right away, then after Dugan used that electric prod…"

Jess clenched her hands. She couldn't have watched that.

Brenna was silent for a while. "She wouldn't have let me leave, would she?" she said finally. "Even if you had signed. The study would just move to the next phase. A new medic might object to Caster's protocols as much as I do, and she wouldn't take that chance. Not when she has me, someone she can control."

"Caster's a monster, lass. To her, we're two lab rats. She said whatever she had to so she could get you into those cuffs."

"She told me you'd be safe." Brenna moved her fingers through the thick softness of Jess's hair. Her eyelashes brushed like feathers against Brenna's skin. "She promised me no one would hurt you again."

They heard the distant banging of a door. Early evening dinner trays were being distributed. This storeroom would not be on the meal cart's delivery schedule.

She studied Jess's aquiline profile by the faint light from the high window. Jess's features carried a simple, almost feral beauty that registered in Brenna's mind with insistent clarity now, whenever she saw her. She needed to hear Jess's rich voice again. To monitor her alertness, she told herself. "Jess, tell me about your village."

"Tristaine?" Jess smiled drowsily. "Tristaine has lots of sky."

"What else?"

"It has a river and a meeting hall. There's a trading post, and cabins, and hundreds of gardens. No computers or televisions. Lots of campfires, though, and fir trees, and vision quests, and stubborn women who can't wake up in the morning without debating it for six hours."

"There really aren't any men in Tristaine?"

"They come and go." Jess was finding it hard to concentrate. The storeroom kept fading in and out. "What are you going to do about Caster, Brenna?"

"I don't know."

Jess lifted her head, listening intently.

"What?"

"Get me up."

Brenna helped Jess sit erect just as a key turned in the lock. Light spilled in from the corridor, and for a moment they were blinded.

"Cybele weeps!" a male voice said. The door closed and darkness fell again. "What in blue hippie hell happened to you two?"

"And you are?" To Brenna's own ears, she sounded absurdly like Charlotte.

"Today, I'm an Amazon's son." The man turned his flashlight on his own face.

It was a stirring gesture, but a mistake. Jodoch's features were pitted and scarred, and they made for a ghoulish image. Brenna slapped a hand to her heart before she recognized the orderly. At the same time she noticed that the beam momentarily illuminated her breasts and that Jodoch averted the light quickly.

"Jode, are they all right?" Jess sounded tense.

"The girls are fine." The big man moved farther into the room and dropped a bulky nylon duffle to the floor. He was younger than Brenna thought at first, close to her own age. She still covered her breasts with one arm, but her pulse was back to normal.

"Camryn wants me to bring her your ear or something, to prove you're still alive. Lordy, Jesstin!" Jodoch pointed the beam briefly on Jess's face again before clicking it off. "I didn't think you could look any worse than you did after the arena."

"Where I handily tromped your butt."

"Pardon me," Brenna said loudly, then leaned closer to Jess. "This is the guy you've got watching out for your friends in the Prison? He's on our day shift, Jesstin!"

"Jode was born in Tristaine." Jess closed her eyes against a wave of dizziness and leaned her shoulder against the wall beside Brenna. "He applied for Clinic staff after I was arrest—"

"Yeah, I'm a plant," Jodoch cut in happily. "Jode the superspy. Pamela says I'm an incredible stud these days, too. Pam's my lucky wife, Brenna."

His shadowed bulk crouched in front of them. They heard him unzip the duffle and rummage inside it. There was a light metallic scraping sound. "Here, Jess, give her this. Pam sent proof that I have Tristainian genes."

A whiff of aromatic steam reached Brenna, and she wrinkled her nose in surprise. "Is that coffee?"

Jess closed her eyes and inhaled with something like reverence. "Not the City swill you call coffee."

"Tristaine's home blend." Jodoch fit Jess's hand around the thermos. "Pam's addicted to it too, now."

Jess swirled the rich brew in her mouth, and its potent richness was more evocative of Tristaine than any photograph. She closed her eyes and felt Dyan's arm against her own as they sat on the wooden steps of the cabin she shared with Shann, drinking coffee and breathing fresh pine air as they watched the sun rise over the far ridge.

"Hey," Brenna said softly.

Jess opened her eyes and passed the thermos to Brenna, the fog beginning to clear from her aching head. "What are you doing here?" she asked Jode. "It's risky enough for—"

"Yeah, and it's getting riskier fast." Jode settled his bulk onto the concrete floor. "Listen, Jess. My new best buddy, Dugan the dick, was crowing like the cock he is at shift change earlier." His brows lowered, making him look like a worried bear. "We're supposed to set up Caster's gym for some kind of marathon clinical test in the morning. And he's all jacked up about…sorry, but he's jacked up because he gets to be the one to hurt Brenna next time. I don't know details, Jesstin, but the two of you are going to get bloody tomorrow. Mostly her. Do you still want to take her with us?"

Brenna's pulse spiked again.

"Are we set at the Prison?" Jess asked.

"Yeah." Jode nodded. "We can get Camryn and Kyla out in six hours, quick and sweet."

Jess sat very still, obviously measuring his words. Jode's large eyes were trusting as he watched her. He seemed to defer to Jess as a matter of course. It was clearly her call.

"Did he say take me with you?" Brenna echoed faintly.

Jess put a hand on Brenna's knee. "How do you know we have enough to bribe Cam and Ky off the cell block?" she asked Jode.

"Barbeler—he's the night guard at the Prison's communal unit—big, quiet kid." Jodoch grinned. "Remember him from the arena? You broke his hand."

Jess groaned. "I broke the hand of the one guard we need to pay off?"

"It's cool, Jess. He's okay with the money we've got so far." Now Jodoch sounded like a teenager trying to convince his big sister. "I think he wants to help. He almost seemed jazzed about this. Barbeler and Pam can get the girls out right after midnight check. Just as soon as we see them safely outta there and headed for the hills, I'll come for you. You can meet Kyla and Camryn at the river well before sunrise."

Brenna was startled. "Jess, you're going to the mountains?"

"Getting Cam and Ky out comes first," Jess said quietly. "Jode. We're a good week early."

"Pam and I are as ready as we would be a week from now!" Jode's voice had risen to a tense squeak. He cleared his throat. "We can get word to Shann. Look, if we don't go with Barbeler now, we might draw someone a lot less cool next week. And Pam and I think it's got to be tonight. By the looks of you two, neither of you can wait three days, let alone a week."

Jess felt Brenna's hand on her arm, and she knew it was true.

"Jess, I'll help you if I can." Brenna pressed Jess's wrist. "Tell me what to do."

"Come with us," Jess said.

Brenna was silent.

"I don't know what kind of life you had in the City, Brenna, but it's gone now." Jess tried to sound reasonable. An Amazon didn't beg. "If we pull this off, you would be the only one left to take the heat. Without Camryn and Kyla and me, Caster's project will be dead in the water. And she'll have a lot to answer for. And a lot of rage. Do you still believe she'll let you quietly resign?"

"No," Brenna said. "Do you believe you can escape up a mountain in six hours? Your heart stopped, Jesstin."

"I can do it." Jess nodded. "With enough decent coffee. And I can do it without you if I have to, but it wouldn't hurt any of us to have a good healer along."

The title registered with Brenna, even through the turmoil of her thoughts.

Jess waited, and so did Jode, through the interminable silence that followed.

Brenna didn't know her decision until she heard herself speak. "I'll go with you."

"We're on. This is great!" Jode slapped his thigh. "Jesstin, you be sure my mother, Jocelyn the Amazon, knows that her son, Jodoch the Man, was the one who rescued you guys. No fair telling Tristaine that Pammy did it all."

"You'll be our hero, Jodey." Jess was almost shivering with relief. She'd thought her heart was going to stop again while she waited for Brenna's answer.

"Great," Jode repeated. He rummaged in the bag. "Pam threw together some warm clothes. I'm no help with sizes. I just told her Brenna's short and you're a tree. We've had the backpacks and camping supplies ready for weeks. Hey." Jode looked up, his flushed face curious. "Hey, Jesstin, if Brenna had said no, would you have bonked her over the head and carried her out of here over your shoulder like a sack of wheat?"

"No, of course not," Jess replied. "Brenna's not a child. She makes her own decisions. But so do I, and if she'd chosen to stay, I wouldn't go either." She felt Brenna's hand on her arm tighten.

"Get out of here, laddy-buck." Jess nudged Jode. "You're late for your shift. We'll see you after midnight. Whoa. Leave the coffee."

CHAPTER SIX

In Amazon lore, taking captives was sometimes a matter of survival. Their modern counterparts had to keep prisoners too, occasionally. While more harmonious than the City, Tristaine wasn't immune to the random criminal impulse.

But when Amazons take prisoners, Jess thought, we not only treat them well—they certainly get better coffee—we also manage to guard them properly, most of the time. In her opinion, the Clinic's lack of visible armed security at night bordered on the absurd.

She paused at an intersection of corridors and slid her hand back, waiting until she felt Brenna's cold fingers brush across her wrist. She then peered carefully around the corner. At the far end of the hall, a lone orderly sat at a battered steel desk, clicking slowly away at a keyboard. A rifle rested against the wall behind his folding chair. Four feet to his right stood the doors that led outside to the Clinic's parking bay. Beyond the doors, Jode's battered van idled in the shadows.

Jess crouched, wincing, and then braced three fingers on the floor until the dizziness lifted. She heard nothing more menacing in the dark hall than the droning hum of the cooling system in the vents above them.

Brenna and Jode crouched behind her. Brenna snugged the collar of her lab coat around her neck. The coat wasn't actually hers, not that hers ever fit, anyway. Jode had found it in the lounge and brought it to her in the hope that anyone who saw them would not immediately remember her fall from Caster's grace.

Jess swiveled and rested her back against the cool plaster. Jode shifted to ease his hips, and his tennis shoe squealed across the tile. Jess lifted an eyebrow at him, but the rattling of the cooler above them would cover the lapse and their muted voices.

"Twenty-five convicted criminals in this facility," Jess murmured, "and only three armed staff at night, covering three widely distant exits?"

"Well, twenty-four of those criminals don't have two gullible Clinic staff willing to unlock their cells," Brenna pointed out. Her teeth were chattering.

"Hey, remember, Cam and Kyla almost caught an entire Prison flat-footed when they tried to bust you out." Jode grunted softly. He was not built for sustained crouching. "City lockups haven't had to cope with anything as mean as Amazons for decades. What now, warrior queen?"

Jess considered. "It's a long walk from here to that desk. We don't need to seem harmless long, but long enough to close the distance."

"Then I suggest we make a harmless *run*, from here to that desk," Brenna whispered.

"Nothing that swashbuckling, sorry." Jess smirked at Brenna. "You'd best enjoy this, lass. You'll never get to do it again."

❖

Swing shift was not so damn hectic that its staff had no time to enter chart notes. Even if the pricks over in Military Research thought they were too holy to do such scut work, there were still half a dozen Civilian orderlies who could type this crap in the afternoons. Grave staff was not being paid enough to go blind doing data entry all blessed night. Swing shift had access to the huge bright monitors at the staff desk.

Malcolm broke off his internal litany and looked up, frowning. He heard the door leading from D wing close, then footsteps. He craned his stiff neck to see the clock on the wall behind him through its wire cage. There was no mention of a one a.m. discharge on his roster.

A large orderly sauntered down the hall, followed by a tall female prisoner with her hands bound behind her. An attractive blond medical tech walked at her side, holding a stunner on the dark woman.

"Yo." The big guy jutted his chin at Malcolm when they were halfway down the corridor. He was swinging a tangle of keys, the possession of which, in Malcolm's view, made Military Research orderlies imagine themselves hefty of penis. "Got a late transfer tonight, compadre."

"First I've heard of it." Malcolm's hand moved to the box on his desk, and Brenna nearly freaked where she stood. One flicked switch would summon two other armed staff.

Jode paused, and for a moment Brenna thought he was frozen. Then he proved himself the son of an Amazon again. "Great. That's great. Another admin fuckup," he grumbled. "Hey, go ahead and call the desk for me, would ya? Have them wake up one of the brass?"

He started walking again, and so did Brenna, nudging Jess along sternly like a good Clinic medic.

"Tell them to call Lorber at home." Jode nodded at Malcolm's hand on the alarm. "Or is there somebody still here this late who can authorize this?"

Malcolm hesitated. Hitting any alarm meant filling out a dozen triplicate forms, even if it turned out there was no real security breach. Mighty Penis here didn't have to assume his glitch was worth that much sweat. He stood, pushing back the folding chair with his thighs and wincing as his spine crackled, and came around the side of the desk.

"You don't have any paperwork? Not any?"

Please don't make us kill him, Brenna thought. She didn't realize she was praying. Let this work. All I want is to get us out of here without anyone getting hurt. But the man's eyes had focused on Jess's face and narrowed. Her status as a Clinic celebrity was proving a definite disadvantage.

"Hey, that's Caster's Amazon." Malcolm's gaze darted to Brenna. "And what's she doing here? That's—"

"Stay low, Bren," Jess whispered.

Malcolm bolted for the rifle, and so did Jess.

Brenna leaped to the right, clearing Jess's path to the desk, and she saw Jode lunge after her. She raced to the desk alarm and cut its power quickly, ensuring that no signal reached the Clinic's other sentries. She whirled as a crash of bodies hit the far wall.

❖

Brenna's teeth were chattering so hard now she could hear them over the rumbling of the van's engine. She helped Jess stretch out on the padded back bench, then squeezed into the cramped floor space behind the driver's seat. She wrapped her arms around her knees to contain her shivering and hoped there were dentists in Tristaine.

Jode bent into the cab of the van and billowed a green canvas tarp over their heads. He had tossed enough painting supplies around to make the back of the van look comfortably messy and nondescript. The musty plastic of the tarp tented neatly above them, an unbroken ceiling stretching from the driver's seat to the van's back doors. Brenna felt a lurch as the big man climbed behind the wheel.

"Can you hear me, Jode?"

The tarp made Jess's voice resonate beside her. Brenna could barely see her in the green shadows, but she could feel her warmth. Her own trembling began to ease.

"Yo." Jode's muffled voice drifted to them. "You two all right back there?"

"Dandy," Jess sighed.

Jode's scarred face had been pale as he eased the tarp over them, but his driving was calm and smooth as the van coasted out of the bay and into the brightly lit lot. "Jesstin?" he rumbled. "Dropping that guy yourself was completely uncalled for, especially seeing as how you were dead just a few hours ago."

"I'm fine, bro."

Fine was a relative term, Brenna thought, trying to see Jess's features through the green gloom. They had left the orderly hog-tied with his own belt in a utility closet, basically whole and safely muzzled. But the diversion had been expensive in terms of Jess's energy.

"I could have taken that guy out, though," Jode asserted.

"I know, Jodey. I got nervous. I'm sorry." Jess lowered her voice, and Brenna leaned in to hear her. "A hundred years, and we're still pampering male egos."

"A hundred years, and butches are still condescending as hell," Brenna replied at normal volume, and Jess winced. "I could have handled him more easily than either of you, Jesstin. And Amazon butches, pardon me, are macha to the point of idiocy—"

"You two lay low," Jode cut in. "Last station coming up."

The tires made a regular thrumming sound as they passed over the succession of steel grids that led to the exit of the Clinic lot, and the final net stretched in their path. The gatekeeper's station housed an armed sentry at all hours.

Brenna rocked against the seat as Jode pulled the lumbering van to a stop, and she steadied Jess on the padded bench.

"Cybele weeps," Jode whispered suddenly.

Ice water deluged Brenna's nerves again, and she gripped Jess's arm. They heard Jode scroll down his side window.

"Nice night," he said to the guard.

"If you're wing nut enough to be awake," Karney replied from the high stool in the gatekeeper's booth.

"Thought you worked day shift, Karney." Jode's mouth was audibly dry.

"Yeah, thought you did, too. Pushing curfew a bit, aren't you?"

Jess closed her eyes. Tristaine still couldn't catch a break. Karney knew very well Jode had no business here this time of night. At the very least he would ask to search the van. She thought they might have to make a run for it, and she wrapped Brenna's arm in one hand to brace them both. She could almost feel Karney's eyes move over the van's dark interior.

"Caster decided a transfer to night watchdog was in order," Karney's sullen voice continued, "after I called in with the flu before her sacred trial this morning. Did Lady Brass Balls kick your schedule to shit, too?"

"And lopped five percent off my pay," Jode improvised. "Grave shift's a bitch and so is she."

Jess smiled at Brenna in the darkness, proud of her brother.

Karney leaned out the window of his booth and spat the last mouthful of dreadful coffee onto the asphalt. "You know Caster's going to crack your nuts, Jodoch, for springing those two."

Gun it, Jess thought, he's calling it in as we sit here. Beside her, Brenna's breath stopped.

"That makes you awful dense," Karney said. "But if anybody thinks every human being with a prick actually is one, they're pretty thick too."

They heard Karney slide his window shut.

A moment later, the van lurched slightly as Jode pulled out of the Clinic's lot and headed north.

Brenna fingered the edge of the tarp aside and watched the spikes of the electrified fence surrounding the Prison tick across the curved window. She shivered again with a relief she knew was not fully warranted yet.

Rain began a tinny patter against the roof of the van. The drizzle would turn the City's streets shining and black. Streets Brenna wouldn't be walking again anytime soon. Her home for all her twenty-odd years. She tried to discern Jess's features more clearly through the murk.

"Jode, what about you and Pam?" Jess shifted stiffly. "You know they'll send Feds to your unit."

"We're not going back." Jode's voice drifted to them. "We'll lie low with one of Pam's buddies until we can bribe up some false papers. We figure Caster's not going to be so hot for our hides that we can't start over eventually."

"Jode." There was real grief in Jess's voice. "You were almost through school."

"So? Show me a Tristainian who needs City schooling to be a good carpenter."

"You were studying electronics, bro, and you loved it."

"Wellup, I love my mama more." Jode's tone was rough with affection. "And Jocelyn of Tristaine would have snatched her baby boy baldheaded if he hadn't helped rescue Shann's little chicks. Don't worry about us, sis."

"On behalf of Tristaine," Jess said, "the chick reference was uncalled for."

Jode snorted cheerfully.

Jess sighed, then her brogue gentled when she spoke to Brenna. "How are you holding up, lass?"

"I'm fine." Brenna hunched her shoulders to try to release the crick in her upper back. The starched stiffness of the lab coat irked her. "I wish I was real drunk."

"You know she'll come after us, Bren."

"Yes, I do."

"Macha to the point of idiocy." Jode chuckled suddenly from the front seat. "I gotta tell Pammy what you said about Amazon butches, Brenna. You two would be best friends. She argues with my mom all the time about stuff like that."

"Tell Pam she *is* an Amazon butch." Jess closed her eyes. Her head was starting to pound again. "Genes have nothing to do with it."

"You better get used to talking genes and politics, Brenna." Jode's grin was in his voice. "They do it all day in Tristaine. Day in. Day out. Day in. That's how Amazons have fun. Weeks at a time. You've been warned."

"As long as they have more of that coffee." Brenna sighed and rested her forehead on her knees.

The steady thrum of the worn tires on the roadway lulled her. She couldn't possibly sleep, but at least the vein-popping tension of the escape was draining away. Brenna lifted her head and focused on the silent woman on the seat above her. "Hey?"

"Hey."

"Your turn. Status report."

"I'm okay." Jess shifted again, trying to find anything resembling comfort on the padded bench. "Well, everything hurts, but I'm functional."

Brenna had to settle for that. "Where are we going, exactly? I mean tonight. Can we get close to Tristaine?"

"Not tonight." Jess rubbed her own shoulder absently. "Tristaine's deep in the mountains, a good week from the City road on foot, even this time of year. We're going to have to hike most of it. Luckily, Kyla and Camryn and I know these hills pretty well."

"Yay," Brenna cheered faintly.

Jess looked down at Brenna, and her rough palm found the back of Brenna's neck and rested there. "You've got to be spooked, lass. This played out much faster than I'd planned. There was no time for much warning."

"I'll be fine." Brenna kept her eyes lowered as if in thought. She tried to quell a new bout of trembling that had risen at the light touch of Jess's hand on her skin.

"Jode will drop us close to a river that the girls know as a meeting place." Jess, as soothed by the thrumming vibrations as Brenna, felt her eyes drift shut. "We'll need to cover some ground before we rest, at least make some inroads up through the foothills."

"You're planning on scaling cliffs? Tonight?" Brenna reached up and rested her fingers against Jess's face. She'd been running a low-grade fever for hours. "You're not getting any cooler, Jess."

"We're under a tarp."

"Jesstin." Brenna's hand found Jess's thigh. "Do you really think you can do this?"

Jess didn't answer for a moment. "I don't know. I can still function, Bren, but I'm pretty rocky. What if I can't?"

Brenna paused. She stroked Jess's leg thoughtfully and then spoke to her as a healer and a friend. "If you can't, I'll help you. We'll get everybody home safe, okay?" She patted her knee in a way that was almost maternal. "Close your eyes, Jess. Get some rest while you can."

The van took the on-ramp for the interstate and moved toward the dark hills.

❖

Jess dozed in a mildly feverish, not-unpleasant haze. Occasionally a jab of pain would surface through it, but mostly she was aware only of cool fingers on her brow, or a light breath stirring her hair. Any images dancing in her mind were softened by Brenna's touch.

Shann bending over her, after her first battle. Jess had not been badly hurt. The only emotion she remembered feeling was a vague relief that the shock of combat hadn't reduced her to tears in front of Tristaine's queen. And the sweetness of seeing Shann's face again, her wise, tender eyes.

Jess awoke to the slow scrunch of tires on sand.

The van rolled to a stop on a rather precarious turnout at the base of the mountains, its fender inches away from a sandy ledge. Below the wash of the van's headlights, the hill sloped steeply until it hit a line of trees, thick ones, difficult to see through at high noon, much less at three a.m. Jess accepted the forearm

Brenna offered to help her rise from the bench and managed to do so without any undignified grunting.

Brenna was carrying more than a woman her size should have been able to lift. The rudimentary aluminum camping frame strapped to her back held blankets, two lanterns, her bag, and enough dried fruit and meat to feed a small family for a week.

She finished tightening a shoulder buckle, then swept her gaze over the van's interior to be sure they had extracted everything Jode had packed for their use. She considered the lab coat, neatly folded on the padded bench. She reached in and laid her hand on its starched whiteness for a moment, but left it behind, a completely impractical garment for a refugee hiking through mountains. The backs of her eyes prickled with tears as she slid the van's door shut.

They would be in Tristaine, in another life, in a week. If Jess's strength held out, Brenna amended, buckling the canvas belt of the pack around her waist. If they weren't caught. If Jess could convince the other two Amazons not to slit her throat for a spy...

"We may not see you again, Jode." Jess clasped the big man's forearm and held it. "Tristaine owes you a lot."

"De nada." Jode grinned. "By the way, I made a lousy orderly, but I was great at filching drug samples. Here." He folded a packet into Jess's hand. "Two tabs of morphia. It was all I could get, so you can't get hurt again."

Jess nodded thanks and slipped them into the breast pocket of her black shirt. "Give our love to Pamela, Jodey."

"Take care, Jesstin."

Jode kissed Jess soundly on her unbruised cheek, then turned and almost walked into Brenna. He squeaked and laid his big hands gently on her shoulders to steady her. "Hey, Brenna. Be careful, and keep my tall friend over there healthy, okay?"

"Thank you, Jode." Brenna rose on her toes and kissed Jode's cheek, surprising him into speechlessness. She smiled up at him crookedly through her spiked bangs, and Jode fell a little in love. "I will. I'll do my best."

The van's headlights illuminated the treacherous slope before them. Jess glanced down the hill, shifting the coils of nylon rope over her shoulder, all Brenna and Jode would let her carry. She raised her head and drank in the spangled expanse of the velvet sky and filled her lungs with chilled mountain air. The urgency of flight gave way, if only briefly, to the euphoria of freedom.

"Have you hiked much, Bren?"

"What other recreation is there on a medic's pay?" Brenna grumbled, adjusting the straps of her heavy backframe. She thought she sounded perfectly collected.

Jess grinned at her, her teeth flashing a ghostly white in the glare of the headlamps. "Then you know to compensate for the weight of your pack when you descend, so you're not thrown off balance, right?"

Jode's duffle bag had provided heavy sweaters and jeans for them both. Brenna worried about Jess's feet. The thin soles of Prison-issue canvas shoes offered little traction over craggy rock. She saw her wince as she drew her arm through the sleeve of one of the windbreakers Pam had packed, and she helped her pull it up over her shoulders.

Jess took Brenna's hand, who let her keep it. She tossed a nod of farewell back to the invisible Jode and sidestepped off the ridge. Brenna followed.

Jess was able to let go of Brenna halfway down. She'd guessed she would be steady on her feet. Above them, they heard the sandy grinding of the van turning back toward the road, and the illumination from its headlights winked out. After their eyes adjusted, the blue moonlight overhead proved an adequate guide.

Jess hesitated as the last sounds of the receding van faded in the cool air. She closed her eyes and drew the sweet spice of pine back into her blood. Even the foothills carried enough remembrance of home to tighten her throat for a moment.

"You okay, Jesstin?" Brenna asked softly.

"Yeah. It's just been a while."

Brenna trusted Jess knew where they were going. Partly because she had no choice, she just concentrated on keeping her balance in the deep sand. The slope leveled off into a grassy area that led into the trees, and Brenna followed Jess silently. They walked side by side, weaving through clumps of freckled aspen. Brenna adjusted to the weight of her pack once they were on even ground.

Brenna threw guarded looks at Jess. She walked a bit stiffly but showed no other outward sign of distress. She tried to keep her mind from listing again the minor injuries Jess had taken in past weeks, in addition to the major traumas.

"We can take a rest stop anytime," she reminded Jess.

Jess gave her a puzzled look. "If we need one. I'd rather wait till we're well off the County road."

Brenna already felt leagues from any tame territory maintained by County Parks, though they had probably covered less than a mile. City hikers were restricted to carefully monitored trails on the outskirts of the foothills, and the forestland they traversed now seemed wild by comparison.

And wildly beautiful. Brenna pulled a deep rush of cool air into her lungs. The shadowed hush that signals predawn filled the fragrant trees around them, and she felt her spirit expanding a little, outside the confines of the City.

Brenna stopped, lifting her head like a young deer scenting the air. "Is that water?"

"Do you hear it, or smell it?" Jess asked her.

Brenna closed her eyes. "Both." She wouldn't have thought she knew what a clean river smelled like, but that faint, tinny scent seemed connected.

"Good, Bren. Your radar's on." Jess continued through the trees. "Watch your footing."

Brenna focused on the root-strewn soil beneath her sneakered feet and on not bonking her head on tree limbs.

She heard the subdued roar of the river long before she saw it. Finally, flecks of white through distant trees registered in her eyes, water moving swiftly over stone. The broad stream emerged as a dark snake cutting through the forest floor in front of them.

"It's all right," Jess called suddenly behind her. "This is Brenna."

Brenna turned, startled, but Jess was studying the surrounding trees, closing the V-neck of her sweater around her throat.

"Who are you?" Brenna faltered. "You mean they're—?"

But Jess was looking over Brenna's shoulder and grinning, so she turned just in time to be spun back around when her shoulder was smacked by a body hurtling past her.

"Hello, Jesstin!"

Brenna's eyes caught a flash of blue cloth as a small woman took a running leap into the arms Jess held open, and she gave a half-grunt, half-laugh as she caught her.

"Good morning, little sister." Jess grinned down at the redhead in her arms. "I missed you too."

Brenna took a step back and walked up against a slender tree. The tree coughed and excused itself, and Brenna whirled.

"Camryn," the tree said.

"Brenna," she stammered, her hand on her breast.

The young Amazon nodded gravely.

Camryn and Kyla were dressed in the same makeshift arrangement of warm clothing that Pam had hastily assembled for them. The green long-sleeved sweater Camryn wore made her look like an earnest young surgeon. She wasn't as broad-shouldered as Jess, but she stood nearly as tall.

Cam's gray eyes moved to Jess. "You're okay?"

"Hello, Camryn." Jess was still grinning as she set Kyla gently on her feet. She was trying not to make a teary spectacle of this reunion. "It looks like you two took good care of each—"

"Uh, no, she's not okay, Cam." Kyla stood on her toes and

cupped Jess's chin, turning her face to try to see her more clearly in the moonlight. "She's not at all. Look at her! What the hell did they do to you back there, Jesstin?"

Kyla pulled down the V-neck of Jess's sweater, revealing the ugly burn at the base of her throat. "Sweet Artemis, adanin."

Cam saw the burn and her mouth fell open. She turned abruptly on Brenna and slapped her, hard.

Brenna's vision exploded in sparks. The blow across her cheek was so unexpected it carried as much impact as a roundhouse right. The backpack threw her off balance, and she dropped heavily to the ground.

Jess moved quickly. She seized Camryn's wrist with steely fingers, and her brogue was deep and cold.

"Is that the ethic Dyan taught, Camryn? To strike a woman down without warning?"

Brenna stared up at Jess, astonished by her fierce eyes, an arctic blue in the moonlight.

Cam stood very still in Jess's grasp. "By the looks of you, Jesstin, I struck an enemy."

"Shann's warned you more than once, little sister, about letting passion cloud your judgment. It's that kind of stupidity that almost earned you and Kyla a life sentence down there."

"Jess," Brenna said.

"You don't know this girl, Camryn, or what's happened between us."

Camryn blinked, and even half-dazed, Brenna could see the muted pain in her eyes.

"Well, we can both see you've been tortured." Kyla's voice shook, but the look she gave Brenna almost flash-fried her where she sat. "She's a Clinic medic, Jesstin. Are you saying she defended you?"

"Kyla, she has a name." Jess released Cam's wrist and extended her hand to Brenna, who took it, and let her pull her to her feet. "Brenna did work at the Clinic. She also saved my life there."

Kyla folded her arms and studied Jess. The low rippling of river over rocks was the only sound for a while. Jess drew in a breath, and Brenna saw her suppress a wince.

"Listen," Jess said quietly, resting her hands on her hips. "I don't care if the three of you are never friends, but we travel together from here on. Kyla, Camryn, you treat Brenna like adanin, because that's what she is to me. Are we clear on that?"

Brenna saw fresh surprise in Cam's expression. "Yes, Jesstin."

Kyla's eyebrows rose, and she looked at Brenna with more curiosity than hostility. She nodded agreement.

Brenna nodded too, then dropped her gaze. The side of her face throbbed hotly. If Cam had led with her fist instead of her open hand, she would probably still be stretched out on the grass.

Camryn and Kyla were close enough to Jess to be sisters. If Samantha had been hurt, Brenna thought, and she believed she was facing the person responsible, she would have used her fist.

"I have something for you, Cam." Jess pulled a small square of plastic-sheathed paper out of her breast pocket. "Jodoch broke into your file and swiped this back. Thank him for it someday."

Cam blinked. She was smiling even before she tilted the small photograph to see its image in the moonlight. She lifted it toward Jess, nodded, and then snapped the picture carefully into her breast pocket.

"Uh, look." Brenna cleared her throat. "Jess, they deserve to know what happened...let's just get this over with."

Jess nodded. "Sure."

"I did work at the Clinic." Brenna met Camryn's eyes. "Jess was my only patient. She was—I allowed her to be hurt there. And I hurt her myself, because I was ordered to. I'm not real proud of that."

Both of the younger Amazons stared at her.

"I don't blame either of you if you don't trust me. I don't much trust me, either. I keep making decisions for the strangest...

anyway." Brenna struggled to focus. "If I travel with you, I'll try not to bring you trouble. And I promise I'll carry my own weight."

Kyla started to speak, but Jess put out a hand and hushed her, studying the sky. Dawn was still an hour away, but a dark blue light had begun to fill the heavens.

"Plane?" Cam asked doubtfully, looking at the rugged terrain around them.

"Helicopter, I think," Jess murmured. That brought their eyes up, but they could see nothing yet.

Brenna could hear it now, a far-off intermittent buzzing, and like the two younger Amazons, she looked automatically at Jess.

Jess's tone was grim. "We've got to find better cover, folks."

❖

All traces of weariness vanished.

Brenna felt adrenaline pump through her legs as they churned up the tree-studded hillside in a widening parallel to the river. They ran in close formation, alert to each other and listening hard for the rotary blade of the chopper.

The burring chatter grew louder, but the strong searchlight beaming down from the mechanical wasp never came near them. They ran under the cover of the trees.

Jesstin signaled a halt half a mile in. Her chest burning, Brenna thought, not just in—up. She stood with the others with her hands on her knees, pulling for breath. The pack on her back hung awkwardly, its weight seemingly doubled in the last stretch.

Jess straightened and listened, her hands on Cam's back and Brenna's. She was as breathless as any of them, but her face alone was streaked with sweat in the predawn air, and Brenna saw her grimace as she straightened. There was no sound except their gasping and the natural cracklings of an awakening forest.

"We need to get under cover before the sun rises," Jess

panted, scanning the sky. "Cam, Dyan always said you could find shelter in a desert salt flat. Take off."

Camryn turned to head up the rocky hillside. Kyla followed her, her smaller form almost visible now in the gray light. She caught up to Cam and pulled her to a stop. She rose on her toes, wrapped her arms around Camryn's neck, and drew her into a passionate kiss.

"Hey," Jess called, and the two young women turned to look back at her.

"Oh. We're bonded, Jess," Kyla called. She smiled, displaying the dimples her big sister Dyan must have teased her about unmercifully. "This might be a chance for a quick make out session or something. Don't tell Shann about us, though. We'll break it to her eventually."

Camryn blushed to the roots of her hair and tugged Kyla gently up the path.

Brenna noted Jess's openmouthed stare. "Wait. Bonded? Does that mean they're—?"

"Hitched." Jess's brows were still arched as she watched the two figures retreat around the bend. "Camryn and Kyla, they're hitched now. And I'm not supposed to tell Shann."

"Shann," Brenna repeated. "Your leader, right?"

"Right. Shann of Tristaine. She who sees and knows all." Jess sighed. "Artemis, take me now."

Brenna smiled, then studied Jess's gleaming face. "How are you?"

Jess scrubbed her hand across her eyes. "We can make some kind of camp by sunrise."

"That's not what I asked." Brenna reached for Jess's forehead, but she tapped her hand away lightly.

"I can make it for another hour, thanks," Jess said. "Stop hovering, Bren."

"Jesstin." Brenna sighed in frustration. "I liked you better when I could tie you down."

Jess grinned.

CHAPTER SEVEN

Camryn found them a broad shelf of sandstone, well protected by trees and shrubbery. It felt safe enough to Brenna, for now. At least Jess had deemed it so, and at the moment she felt almost blindly willing to follow her instinct.

She tried to help gather fuel for a fire, but Jess declined her first armload as a kind of wood that gave off too much smoke. She fared better assisting Camryn with what Jess called a perimeter search, but the Amazons declined wearily when she offered further assistance in setting up camp. Brenna didn't protest much. She was spent.

She lowered herself to the ground and eased back against a slab of rock. Its cool base pillowed the persistent ache in the small of her back as she watched the sun complete its slow push over the eastern ridge. Finding reassurance in night's end was primitive superstition, but Brenna took her comfort in any form she found it, and she relished the dawn.

She studied the three Tristainians as they finished laying out their gear. There was affection in the easy way the women touched in passing, the same kind of physical grace notes she had always shared with her sister, and no one else. *Sammy*, Brenna thought. She closed her eyes.

"Jess is probably going to send us off in a minute."

Brenna lifted her head as Kyla settled cross-legged beside her. "What's that?"

"Jess. She's going to banish us again." Kyla's tone was confiding and friendly. She had the fresh, clear face of a young woman just leaving childhood behind, but Brenna noted the fine lines around her eyes, and she was entirely too thin. This girl had lost a sister and spent weeks in a Federal Prison. Both experiences had aged Kyla beyond her years.

"Personally, I think it's because Jess wants to be alone with you," Kyla suggested. "But Cam says it's because Jess doesn't want to watch us make out. Actually, I think Cam's sort of uncomfortable kissing me in front of Jess. What do you think?"

"Well, let's see." Brenna watched Jess break kindling over her knee, wincing at the same time she did. "I think she's still trying to cope with the fact that you two are together, period. That you've blended?"

"Bonded." Kyla snickered, and so did Brenna.

"Bonded, right. She seemed surprised to hear it."

"Well, we weren't when they transferred Jess to the Clinic." Kyla looked at Camryn with dreaming eyes. "Cam and I have been adanin since we were kids. We were going to be adonai eventually, no matter what. But once they took Jess, and we were alone together…we were scared most of the time."

Brenna said nothing. She was surprised by a hand covering her own.

"I wasn't jabbing you, Brenna. You weren't the one calling the shots back in that place. I know that."

Brenna nodded.

"Jess called you adanin," Kyla said. She smiled tentatively. "Do you know what that means?"

"I was kind of surprised when she said it. I thought it only applied to women from Tristaine."

"It means sister." Kyla nudged her with her shoulder. "Like with a capital S. It's not a word we apply to every woman, not even every woman in Tristaine. And very few outside it. Adonai is a whole other word, by the way. That's what Cam and I are now."

Brenna nodded again. "And what do you think I'll be to you, Ky? Friend or foe?"

Kyla appraised her frankly. "I don't know yet," she said finally. "Cam still doesn't trust you. I think she's sorry she hit you, but she's not going to apologize for it anytime soon."

"Okay." Brenna turned her head against the rock to look at her. "That's Camryn. What do you think?"

"I think that, except for Jess, you must feel all alone out here, and that's got to be hard." Kyla's eyes were compassionate as well as keen, and Brenna felt an odd tightness in her throat.

"We won't let anything happen to you, Brenna. Okay? Please don't worry. Even Cam, she'll fight anybody for you, now that Jess has named you adanin. That makes you our sister in a way, too."

Brenna smiled thanks, then glanced down at the ill-fitting clothes they both wore. "Does this mean I can borrow your outfits?"

Kyla let out a bark of infectious laughter.

They sat in companionable silence watching the sun crest the ridge.

"We have to find something besides dehydrated bacon fat for breakfast." Jess sighed, slinging down a last stack of kindling. "Camryn, Ky, see what you can dig up."

"See, make out opportunity," Kyla murmured to Brenna as she pushed herself to her feet.

Brenna noted that Camryn didn't look at her as she took Kyla's hand.

"Remember, we've lost the cover of night," Jess called after them, straightening slowly from her crouch by the firepot. "Keep under cover, and stay within whistle call."

"We hear and obey, oh liege." Kyla waved.

Jess waited until their soft footfalls faded in the morning air, then walked to the neat stack of backpacks and removed an armload of blankets. She reached for the canteen in Camryn's frame, but Brenna's hand darted in ahead of hers and lifted it out.

"Is there some reason you don't want those two to know you're out on your feet?" Brenna sounded annoyed, which concealed her worry. She twisted the cap off the canteen and handed it to Jess.

Jess swirled the cool water on her tongue. "Don't exaggerate, Brenna."

"All right, I won't exaggerate if you won't be a macha butch idiot," Brenna said politely.

She led Jess over to a protected corner of the rock shelf and snapped one of the blankets out over the shaded stone. Jess lowered herself onto it stiffly and rested her stinging back gingerly against the rock. Brenna rummaged through her own pack until she found her medical kit.

Jess eyed the small black case warily. "You brought needles out here?"

"Just the big, thick, dull ones." Brenna slipped a thermostrip from its packet and tapped it on Jess's lower lip until she accepted it glumly.

Jess's face was haggard, the cobalt blue of her eyes muted to the stormy indigo of the sea. Brenna didn't need the strip to know the fever had returned. The brush of her fingers down the side of Jess's face told her that much. She measured her pulse at the throat.

Funny how you could feel defenses lowering, Jess thought, like a fence of shields around you dropping one by one. Brenna's cool fingers on her skin ushered a pleasant tingle through Jess's chest. Her breath was soft and warm on her throat.

Brenna checked the thermostrip to confirm the verdict. "You're heating up again. Why don't you crash for a while? We'll wake you when breakfast is ready."

"Someone needs to stand watch," Jess mumbled.

"I will, until the kids get back." Brenna smiled and shook her head. "Listen to me. I sound like a mother."

"Shann says that's what being adanin does to you."

"Do you want one of those painkillers?"

Jess shook her head, eyes closed. "Probably need it more tonight, before we move."

"Jesstin." Brenna hesitated. "Why did you tell Kyla and Camryn that I saved your life? Did you mean the CPR, after you—?"

"You wouldn't let me die. You called me back."

Brenna had no response to that. She checked the healing burn at the base of Jess's throat, then opened her shirt to examine her bruised ribs. Her cool hands moved carefully over her tender side, then slipped the shirt down one of Jess's muscular arms. "Here, lean. Best let me check your back while we have some privacy."

"It's better. Just don't poke anything."

"No poking," Brenna promised. The welts and whip cuts striping Jess's back were less livid but still warm and tender to the touch. She applied a mild salve with careful fingers, then eased the cloth back in place.

"I was wrong, Jess."

Jess blinked and focused on Brenna's still face. "About what?"

"I hadn't admitted that yet. Out loud or to you. I've been saying it in my head for weeks." Brenna stared out over the sandstone shelf. "I was wrong to believe Caster. I closed off all my instincts…what I knew was right, for way too long. I let her convince me that what was happening to you was necessary, that I had to let you be hurt. Surviving was everything to me, Jess. And I am so…bloody sorry."

"I am too. Sorry we both had to go through it." Jess's voice was gentle. "That part's over now, Bren."

Brenna nodded and played with the trailing edge of Jess's shirttail. "Do you think we'll ever get past it?"

"Do you think you'll ever allow my touch?"

Brenna's eyes rose to her face, filled with such lost sadness Jess felt every shield she'd ever forged topple like dominoes.

"How can you want me." The way Brenna said it, it wasn't a question. "I'm pure City, Jesstin. I was born there. I've lived there all my life."

"And I was born in Tristaine." Jess winced and eased herself higher against the stone. "I've had the blessings of choice, and I've chosen you. You were never the City's, Bren. You wouldn't be here now if you were."

Jess took her hand, and Brenna felt a quiver of subterranean thirst.

It had been there between them, since the first night in the Clinic's detention cell, this odd quickening in the blood. At first it had been possible for Brenna to ignore it in the haze created by duty and anguish and alcohol. But the Clinic and its white lab coats were far away from this morning's shaded ledge.

She felt her body relaxing against Jess's warm side. The strength left her arms as she leaned into her and rested her head carefully on her bare breast.

Jess swallowed and heard the dry crackling in her throat in spite of the water she drank minutes before. She stared down into the soft hair at her throat, Brenna's sweet weight keeping her safely anchored to the rock. She felt the light brush of eyelashes on her breast as Brenna closed her eyes, and she let out a shaking sigh.

Brenna rested. She felt the cadence of her own pulse slow and settle into the gentle, steady rhythm throbbing beneath her cheek. The beat was still there, still strong. They all were, in spite of Caster's worst.

❖

"I miss storyfires." Kyla smiled dreamily, staring into crackling flames in the center of their circle. "Also that wine Constance makes from our vineyard."

"Jocelyn's bread." Camryn was stretched out on her back, her long fingers twined beneath her head. "Night hunts."

"Real coffee," Jess added.

"My dogs." Kyla peered at her hand, frowning. "You know there's not a single dog in the City? And they call us barbarians."

"Rae's mutton stew." Camryn's voice was reverent.

"Morning swims in the lake," Kyla said.

"Real coffee," Jess sighed.

Kyla snorted and slapped Jess's thigh.

Kyla was more demonstrative than either of Tristaine's warriors, Brenna noted, but all three Amazons clearly relished being within hand's reach again. Kyla and Camryn were hungry for Jess and she for them. They needed to hear each other's voices and share laughter again and breathe the same free air.

A visible weight had lifted from Jess's shoulders, and the eyes that had been so guarded behind Clinic walls sparked with life in her sisters' company. Those eyes still held a glassy sheen, but the food seemed to have beaten back Jess's fever for now.

They were finishing a light meal of the dried jerky Jodoch supplied and the fresh berries Cam and Kyla found by the river. Brenna had to resist urging more on the two youngest in their party. Camryn was as painfully thin as Kyla after weeks on Prison rations. There had been little talk of their time there, or of Jess's tenure in the Clinic, for which Brenna was grateful.

"What else?" Even sitting in this close circle, Brenna was keenly aware of her outsider status, but these memories of Tristaine called to her nonetheless.

"Archery tournaments," Jess offered. "Creaming Camryn at archery tournaments."

"Racing horses." Camryn grinned. "Watching Jess get dumped racing horses. Kyla, will you stop messing with that?"

"Can't help it." Kyla was scowling at her palm again.

"Here, you're just making it worse." Cam pulled Kyla's hand to her knee, but she snatched it back.

"You can't get it, Cam. You don't have any fingernails left after clearing fields for—"

"I'm just looking at it."

"That's not looking, that's squeezing. Camryn, *ow*, dang it!"

"You two sounded exactly like this when you were five," Jess complained. "What's the problem?"

"Oh, brains here," Camryn jutted her chin at Kyla, "grabbed hold of a thorn bush to pull herself out of a ditch, and now she's got this big bloody spike in her hand."

"Spike," Kyla groaned. "Camryn, it's a sticker. I have a sticker in my hand," she told Jess.

"Want me to take a look?" Brenna asked Kyla. "I'm pretty good with spikes."

"We can manage," Cam said. "Thanks."

"It's up to you, adanin," Jess told them. "But I'd think if you could manage, it would be out by now."

Brenna shifted over to sit closer to Kyla. "I promise not to cut it off."

"Yeah, I guess we better." Kyla shook out her stinging hand. "Thanks, Bren."

Camryn moved a few inches to make room for Brenna, her eyes downcast.

"Let's see." Brenna lifted the girl's hand into her lap and tilted her palm toward the light. The embedded thorn was an angry darkness in the pad at the base of her thumb. "Uh, Camryn's right. That's a spike."

Kyla groaned again.

"Maybe you should just put something on it." Cam peered over Kyla's shoulder. "Leave it for Shann to dig out."

"Good idea," Kyla said quickly.

"We won't see Shann for days, Ky," Jess reminded them. "Maybe weeks."

"This really should come out now." Brenna tipped Kyla's hand to see the reddened area more clearly. "Camryn, would you bring me my kit? It's in the blue pack."

Cam unwound her long limbs reluctantly and got to her feet.

"Shann would probably just put a poultice on it," Kyla said feebly.

"Shann would go after you with her rusty dagger," Jess

corrected. "Have courage, lass. Brenna's got a skilled and tender touch."

Brenna accepted her kit from Camryn with a smile of thanks and began arranging her supplies. After sterilizing a needle and tweezers, she dabbed a mild cleanser onto a folded cloth and patted it gently across the pad. The girl's hands could have belonged to a dishwasher twice her age, Brenna noted. Exposure to the harsh detergents of the Prison's kitchen had left them blanched and rough.

Kyla was emitting a series of sighs, her eyes fixed on the distant horizon in preparation for the agony to come. Jess curbed a smile, but Camryn shifted closer to her lover and clasped her other hand tightly.

"I hate needles," Kyla explained to Brenna. "Also pain of any kind."

"Runs in the family." Jess linked her long fingers around one raised knee and grinned at Kyla. "Remember when Dyan fell butt first into that rosebush last spring?"

Camryn's face lit up. "Man, I didn't think that many thorns could stick in one human ass! She bellowed like a speared boar."

"Shann had to chase her around their cabin three times, waving her pliers," Kyla added, and she was grinning too. Their laughter was healing.

Brenna patted Kyla's wrist. "You all right?"

"Oh, sure." Kyla dried her eyes with the back of her free hand. "Just memories, you know. It's okay, Brenna, I'm ready. Go ahead."

"I'm done." Brenna patted Kyla's palm with the cleanser. "Your spike came out around the time Dyan fell into the bush."

"Get *out*!" Kyla stared at her hand, pop-eyed, then showed it to Camryn. "Brenna, you're a genius!"

Camryn's eyebrows arched.

"Let me slap on a Band-Aid. You'll want to keep it clean." Brenna smoothed the small bandage in place deftly. "I trust all

Amazons don't make their medics psychotic, like your strange friend over there."

The fond light in Jess's gaze warmed Brenna better than the weak rays of the sun, but her increasing pallor was a reminder of how long it had been since any of them had any real sleep.

Jess seemed to read her mind and climbed painfully to her feet. "We've got ground to cover tonight. Let's get some rest."

"I don't want to close my eyes on you." Kyla slipped her arms around Jess's waist and pulled her close. "I'm afraid you'll disappear again."

"I'll be here when you wake, adanin." Jess winced as Kyla's arms tightened, but she rested her lips in the girl's hair. "I'll take first watch, Camryn, if you'll spell me after—"

"I'll take first, Jess." Camryn shook out another blanket over the shaded rock to form a pallet for her and Kyla. "Old women need their sleep."

Jess groaned, but didn't protest.

"You can tap me next," Brenna offered. "If standing watch just means screaming my head off if I see anything, I can do that."

Camryn glanced at Jess, who nodded.

Their packs held only so much room for blankets. It was share them or sleep on dusty stone. Brenna surreptitiously helped Jess settle on the second pallet, then lowered herself next to her, trembling with fatigue. She suppressed a moan as she stretched out, trying to find a position her aching muscles would tolerate.

"This is like trying to sleep on a riverbank beside a flopping trout," Jess griped.

"Well, now I know how one feels," Brenna muttered. She rolled over carefully and blinked with surprise to see Cam's sneaker an inch from her nose. She craned her neck to see the serious face above them.

"Jesstin, I found a ledge with good sightlines above that brush there. You can crash. Nothing's getting within a mile of us without being seen."

"Tristaine has no sharper eyes," Jess said. "I'll sleep well, Cam."

"Good. Uh, thanks, Brenna," Camryn mumbled. "For Ky's hand."

Brenna smiled. "Sure, Camryn. Glad I could help."

She was asleep before Camryn mounted the ledge.

❖

Sometime after the sun crested noon and began its journey west, Jess moaned in her sleep.

Cam frowned and lifted herself from the stone lip of the shelf where she stood watch, then saw that the woman sleeping beside Jess had awakened at the low sound.

Camryn watched Brenna feel her sister's face, then her hands. Jess lay on her side, gripped by such vicious chills Cam could see her shaking from the ledge. Brenna pushed down the blanket, then opened Jess's shirt. She unbuttoned her own green sweater and lay down again, resting her bare breasts against Jess's to warm her. She slipped a supporting arm around her shoulders as she pulled up the blanket to cover them both. Brenna rested her head on Jess's shoulder.

Camryn watched them silently for a while, then returned to her watch.

❖

The two stallions charged each other, trumpeting screams of rage that sounded almost human. They met in a terrible crash of flashing teeth and powerful, churning kicks, shattering the peace of the pasture with the fury of their battle. Around them, the herd milled in fearful chaos, raising clouds of dust as their bodies thudded together, their hooves trampling the sparse grass in panic.

Brenna awoke instantly, every vestige of sleep banished in one quick, shivering burst of alarm. Her hand reached immediately for Jess, but swept across an empty blanket.

"Jesstin's gone, Brenna." Camryn pushed herself away from the rock wall and went to her, puzzled by her expression.

"W-where is she?"

"Don't freak. I don't mean gone gone." Camryn glanced over her shoulder at Kyla, still sleeping yards away. She turned back to Brenna, then averted her gaze. "I thought I heard something. Some kind of motor. I woke Jess, and she went to check it out."

"I'd better check *her* out." Brenna realized the young Amazon was studiously avoiding looking at her bare breasts, and she blushed slightly as she pulled down her shirt to cover them.

"No need, Brenna. Jess is pretty careful."

"Yeah, I know. But she's been through a lot." She groped for her shoes beneath the blankets, then climbed to her feet.

And sat down again with an ungainly thump. Every muscle in Brenna's body screamed regret for last night's uphill flight with a full pack. She was certain for a moment that she would throw up, but the nausea receded as quickly as it hit. Chills racked her, and her hands shook. The back of her throat was raw and ached for the sharp bite of whiskey.

"Hey. You all right?" Cam frowned, her hand almost touching Brenna's head before she folded her arms. "You look worse than Jess did, and that was pretty bad."

"Just waking up," Brenna managed. "This is me in the morning." She laced her shoes, shaking the last of the dream from her mind. "Which way did she go?"

"The sound came from the north." Cam nodded toward the trees. "Uh, don't get lost out there, all right? If you don't find her fast, come back and we'll regroup."

They had laid camp that morning barely out of the foothills, not far west of the river that had been their rendezvous point. To reach the rock shelf, they'd had to travel a long stretch through open land, and Brenna looked back over that vista now. She scanned the sunlit reaches of the foothills, searching, the crisp air clearing the fog from her head. She heard a splashing sound and turned quickly, then plowed through a barrier of hedge brush.

The distant figure was kneeling in the frigid current of the stream, which swirled and tumbled around her thighs. Jess had obviously immersed herself fully more than once, and her hair hung in soaked strands around her face and throat. Brenna stared at her from the riverbank, appalled.

Her fever must have rocketed while they slept, Brenna thought. There was no telling how rational Jess's thinking had been when she sought out the icy water. She was trying to cool her body fast, a primitive and dangerous instinct. She was apparently unconcerned that she was subjecting her weakened system to a horrendous shock, and completely in the open beneath a cloudless blue sky.

"Jesstin!" Brenna gave the empty heavens a fast search, and then she jumped off the shallow bank and into the river. She staggered when her sneakered feet hit the smooth rocks of the riverbed, but her athlete's reflexes steadied her. Her ankles went numb with the immediate, stinging cold of the water, small waves slapping up to her knees.

"Jess!" Brenna slogged through the gentle current, alarmed that Jess didn't seem to hear her. "Hey, look at me!"

Jess leaned forward to lower her head completely beneath the chilled, dancing water again. Brenna reached her while her head was still submerged, and at first she thought Jess was merely startled.

Her reaction to the touch of Brenna's hands on her back was galvanic. She reared up on her knees like a branded stallion, slinging jets of water from her black hair, and there was nothing sane in her face.

"Jess, it's me!" Brenna gasped. She fell to her knees in the water and gripped Jess's arms. "You idiot! I don't care how strong you are, your heart can't take—"

Jess shook off her hands effortlessly and clasped her wrists.

With both of them kneeling, she towered over Brenna. A greedy light ignited her features.

"Every time you touched me." Jess's brogue was soft. "Whenever I felt your fingers on my skin, sweet Brenna, I felt my mouth on you."

"Jesstin, make sense." Brenna pulled one hand free and cupped the back of Jess's neck. "That fever might—"

Jess lunged to her feet, carrying Brenna with her. Pure instinct reigned then, on both sides. Brenna fought to free herself, and Jess fought to carry her to the bank. Jess was bigger, but it took all of her strength to haul Brenna out of the river and up the muddy bank.

Jess had been away far too long. She was going home.

She threw Brenna's struggling body down in the grass and stood over her, one foot on either side of her waist. "I'll not break my word, Brenna. If you still refuse my touch, say so now."

The rational tone seemed to belong to a different woman. The one standing over Brenna knelt in the grass by her side and began to strip her. She bared the gold mound between her thighs first. Then she snatched her sweater open, baring her full breasts.

"I felt it the first time you touched me, and so did you." Jess pushed Brenna's knees apart with gentle, but inexorable strength. "Your touch was as welcome and dear to me as sunlight, Brenna."

Jess stared down at her soft, exposed center. Brenna moaned and turned her head on the grass, feeling that gaze on her labia as palpably as heat. Abruptly, Jess snugged her cold, wet palm against her quivering cleft, and the moan ended in a cry of shock. But Brenna made no move to cover herself.

Brenna had never traveled here. She hadn't known this place existed. She didn't know herself here, but she wasn't afraid. She couldn't take her eyes off the austere beauty of Jess's face.

"I've come for you, lass." The brogue rendered Jess's voice as soft as moss. "I'm taking you home."

Jess's gaze fastened for a long moment on Brenna's shuddering breasts, then moved lower. Her long fingers began stroking her wetness.

"Jess," Brenna gasped. The fingers dancing slowly in her cleft hesitated, but when Brenna said nothing more, they continued their languorous twirling.

Jess entered Brenna carefully, slowly, unaware of the tears blurring her vision. That she was capable of such self-restraint was testament to Dyan's rigorous insistence on self-discipline. Like all Tristaine's warriors, Jesstin had had her moments of youthful rebellion against such restrictions. Now, she used that inner strength to protect her lover against her own raging blood. She took her time, working Brenna gently, allowing small muscles to relax, listening to her hitching breathing to gauge her rising desire, then moving deeper.

Brenna lifted herself briefly on her heels as Jess sank in fully, the dark, swirling pleasure spiking so quickly she couldn't suppress her reaction in spite of her efforts. "Damn you, Jesstin," she whispered.

"I wanted you, every time you looked at me." Jess's voice grew more even as she settled into a rhythm, her thumb circling gently over Brenna's tight center, her long fingers delving in and out in skilled cadence.

Brenna moaned softly, and Jess's eyes moved to her flushed face. "In the storeroom. When I saw your face above me. I wanted you even then, adanin, and your eyes held the same light."

Brenna emitted another sound, more like a groan, and Jess's words cut off as her own arousal coursed higher. She had to lower her head to Brenna's stomach for a moment, but her fingers never stopped their gentle, relentless attack.

Brenna's belly flooded with heat, and a fiery pleasure coursed through her nipples and returned to simmer in her loins. She tried again to moan out a protest, but all that emerged this time was Jess's name. Brenna knew her movements were changing; she had begun undulating beneath the tall form pinning her. When Jess raised her head, she saw that Brenna's lidded eyes were filling with need.

"You've only known me powerless, Bren. Don't make the mistake of believing me so now."

She covered Brenna's mouth with her free hand. Then she bent, fastened her lips around her protruding clitoris, and nibbled it gently.

Climax hit Brenna so fast and fiercely she convulsed with it. Her hoarse scream was drowned by Jess's hand over her mouth, but her lips opened against her palm as she screamed again.

The spasms in Brenna's center began to subside, and Jess released her. After a moment, she worked her fingers slowly and gently from between Brenna's splayed legs, leaving her emptied.

Jess climbed to her feet in stages. She looked down at Brenna silently, her hair and black clothing still dripping with river water. She didn't move to help her stand, and Brenna did not ask her assistance.

Brenna adjusted her clothing slowly and got to her feet. They studied each other in the birdsong silence. Jess regarded her calmly, and her expressive features held no regret.

And Brenna discovered she felt none. Against all logic, she was filled with a shimmering peace. She wondered again if she was losing her sanity.

Jess's head lifted imperceptibly when Cam's whistle reached them from the other side of the trees. The low, musical note held apprehension, and Jess answered at once, with a trilling whistle of assurance. A moment later, a third whistle acknowledged her.

Jess looked back at Brenna and then at the open land around them. Her expression changed, her eyes growing dark. "I could have brought a search party down on all of us."

"It was the fever," Brenna said gently. She was still trembling. "You've been...out of your head, Jess."

Jess stared at her.

"You didn't hurt me," Brenna added.

"I know that."

"Jess, you were delirious."

"No, I wasn't. Not then. My fever broke in the stream, Brenna." She nodded toward the trees. "Let's get under cover."

Brenna followed her into a sparse copse of aspen. Jess walked soundlessly over the leaf-strewn ground, and Brenna tried to step in her footprints, to achieve equal stealth. Soon she was hopping from print to print, and annoyance burgeoned in her chest.

"Slow down, Jesstin."

Jess ignored her.

"Hey." Brenna trotted a few steps and caught her arm. "Walking, at any speed, is not particularly comfortable for me at this time. You're being rude, Jess."

That seemed to sting. Jess turned back and rested her hands on her hips.

"Look, I haven't mastered the whole Amazon-stoic thing, just yet." Brenna folded her arms, shivering with the chill the mountain breeze sent through her damp clothes. "You just blew the top of my head off back there, Jesstin. A moment to collect my thoughts is not too much to ask."

"Can't you collect while we—?"

"No. Listen, you had plenty to say a few minutes ago, and I heard you out. Now it's my turn." Brenna stepped closer to Jess, searching her face. "You were right. You weren't alone down there, in what you were feeling. I've dreamed about you every night since we met. I saw your face every time I closed my eyes. You haunted me, Jess."

Jess closed the distance between them, until Brenna's breasts nestled beneath her own. She warmed Brenna's arms with her hands until she stopped shivering.

"And we still have some unfinished business." Brenna curled a hand beneath Jess's hair and cupped her neck. "Now, when we're both more or less sane. We were rudely interrupted the first time."

Jess bent her head and then hesitated, her lips a mere inch from Brenna's. Brenna rose on her toes and met her, and their mouths blended in a rush of exhaled sighs. Their heat was more tender than passionate now, a glowing ember rather than flame. Brenna trailed her fingers down the side of Jess's face in something like wonder.

Camryn's second whistle parted them.

Jess lifted her head, her eyes filled with bemused regret. "We'll have time," she promised. "We've got to find safety first."

Brenna nodded. Jess offered her hand, and she took it. They walked together deeper into the trees.

❖

Jess stalked silently into the camp, past the worried scrutiny of Camryn and Kyla, and on to their packs. She rummaged in Brenna's kit and withdrew a small packet.

Kyla glanced at Brenna's damp jeans as she joined them and put a questioning hand on her wrist. Brenna shook her head and nodded toward Jess. They watched her dry-swallow a capsule, then pull some folded clothing from the pack.

Jess went to Brenna and handed her a stack of dry clothes. Her step on the sandstone wasn't quite steady. The abrupt retreat of the fever left her feeling temporarily as weak as a pup. And cold. And disoriented. In addition to all the other things Jess was feeling, none of which she had time for now.

"All right." Jess rested her hands on her hips and regarded Kyla and Camryn. "Physically, I'm rockier than I let on. I'm going to be fine, but I'm not at my best. Okay?"

"Okay." Kyla nodded.

"Right now I can travel well enough, and fight if necessary. But if the fever kicks in again, I might get spacey." Jess appraised them for a moment. "The three of you can take me if you have to. Act fast if need be, Cam. Don't fuck around."

Cam swallowed visibly. "Okay, Jesstin."

Kyla nudged Brenna and lifted her eyebrows. Brenna shrugged and nodded.

They struck camp at sunset.

CHAPTER EIGHT

They hiked through a misting rain for the first two hours. The terrain was rocky forestland in the middle of the wet season, and slogging through mud puddles became routine. The clouds began to disperse an hour after dark fell in full, and lacework glimpses of stars appeared overhead.

"I'll show you in the morning. Moonlight's lousy for this." Kyla was holding up the tail of her shirt for Brenna, who was squinting at the intricate design etched into the skin of her belly. "It's just my guild's crest and the symbol for Tristaine. Pretty, though, huh?"

"It's amazing." Brenna straightened, and she and Ky trotted a few steps to catch up to Jess and Camryn. "Jess's glyph's on her shoulder, but yours…"

"Yeah, they can be anywhere. You should see Cam's, Brenna. It's really gorgeous."

"Pass," Camryn said stolidly, skirting a snarl of roots in their path.

Kyla snickered. "She won't show you because she put hers smack between her two warriorly breasts. But Cam's glyph has the warrior's arrow, just like you've seen on Jess's shoulder, and Tristaine's stars, which all of us have."

Brenna remembered the scattering of lights across Jess's design. "Are Tristaine's stars up there tonight?"

"Should be." Kyla trotted a few yards up a hill and spun in a slow circle, her eyes trained on the sky. "Come on. Gaia knows I've waited long enough for a sky fix," she muttered. She began walking backwards as the others reached her, squinting at the heavens.

"A wise warrior," Jess lectured Camryn, "is never distracted. She keeps her eyes level, her senses focused on her surroundings."

"Well, I'm not a warrior." Kyla laughed, catching herself lightly on Brenna's shoulder as she stumbled. "And I've been shut in too dang long, so leave me alone."

The star field opened gradually above them, swatches of cloud drifting to reveal brilliant pinpricks of light.

"There's Anath," Kyla said, pointing for Brenna, who turned to look too. "Bloody war goddess, Brenna. She's great! And that cluster over there, they're the Ghost Dancers, spirits of the first Amazon clan in the Far East."

Jess and Camryn both gave in to temptation, and the four women stood in a close group, searching the skies. Jess wrapped her long arm around Brenna's waist as naturally as the cool night air brushed her skin, and she found herself relaxing against her.

"Where'd they go?" Camryn was scowling as she craned her neck. "Shouldn't they be right there?"

"They are," Kyla said. "There's just still cloud cover over—no, look. There they are!"

Brenna followed her pointing finger and saw one of the few constellations she recognized. Astronomy wasn't a State-sanctioned science. The City's light made much of the night sky unreadable, but tonight the star cluster known as Caesar sparkled brilliantly against a bed of ebony. The seven stars composing the Roman dictator's reclining figure could be seen even through the City's murky haze most of the year.

"Those Seven Sisters are the Adanin, Brenna." Kyla's face was luminous in the moonlight. "They're the Amazons who founded Tristaine. When the last of them lay dying, she wept at the thought of leaving our village without the wise guidance of the original seven. So Artemis set Kimba and her sisters in the sky, so they could counsel us forever."

"Kimba, Julia, Jade, Beatrice, Killian..." Camryn's bony finger moved. "Wai Yau, and Constance."

"That's Beatrice," Jess corrected. "That's Constance."

"Don't think so." Camryn shook her head. "I've got the sharpest eyes in Tristaine."

"They're beautiful," Brenna said. "I've never seen them before."

"Every woman in Tristaine chooses one of the seven Adanin as her personal guardian." Jess stroked Brenna's hair. "She becomes one of her Mothers, the goddesses she prays to."

"How do you choose one?" Brenna fixed on the small star glittering on the western edge of the cluster. "I mean, is there some system?"

"The Adanin counsel our seven guilds." Kyla leaned back into Camryn. "Wai Yau guides our mothers, Kimba, our warriors and hunters. Our gardeners choose Beatrice, artists have Jade, and weavers and other tradeswomen follow Constance."

"You would be Killian's, Bren." Jess showed Brenna the shining star near the center of the cluster. "She watches over Shann's guild, Tristaine's healers."

Brenna smiled, but her eyes lingered on the isolated spark of light in the west. "Who in Tristaine follows Julia?"

"Julia," Kyla repeated, grinning. "Isn't she gorgeous? As far as we know, her line has completely died out, but she was Tristaine's first great spiritual guide. She counsels our historians and seers."

"Seers." Brenna felt deflated. "You mean psychics?"

Camryn tittered. "Yeah, Julia must be kind of lonely up there. Tristaine's never had one."

"Shann says that some women are chosen by their Adanin." Jess's breath stirred Brenna's hair. "That's not always lucky, according to our legends, but it's always an honor."

Then Brenna felt Jess go still behind her. She looked up at her questioningly.

"Did you hear that?" Kyla asked quietly.

Then Brenna heard it too, an odd, muted crackling sound far in the distance.

"North or east?" Camryn's eyes darted across the horizon.

"North. Listen." Jess put a quieting hand on Kyla's shoulder, and Brenna strained her ears, but heard only the chirping of crickets. Apparently the others detected nothing else that might prove more menacing, because after a moment Jess relaxed.

"I'd feel better if we checked it out." Jess took the rope from Camryn and secured it over her shoulder. "I'll take Kyla and try for a higher vantage point. You two, keep to the route. We'll meet you at the north end of the valley. Camryn, you know the rock formations in the clearing on the north side?"

Camryn nodded. "About a mile, maybe less."

"Look for us there." Jess looked at Brenna and smiled reassurance. "Keep a sharp eye. It was probably an animal, but we need to be sure."

"Yeah, it's a harmless grizzly or something," Brenna suggested faintly.

Jess grinned. "We'll be careful."

"Bye." Kyla stood on her toes and gave Camryn's cheek a smacking kiss. "Come on, Jesstin. A warrior doesn't sit on her butt when there's varmints to track."

❖

Brenna and Camryn hiked side by side in a courteous but strained silence. Cam did crack a smile when Kyla unleashed an especially elaborate "all's well" whistle, so they shared that moment.

Brenna found herself talking to Samantha again, in her mind. Something about Kyla seemed to keep her sister just beneath the surface of her awareness. She tried to explain things to Sam and say good-bye.

She was startled by the white, neatly folded handkerchief that appeared before her. Brenna smiled reluctantly, snatched it, and blew her nose.

"You can keep that," Cam said gravely.

"Thanks, I will." Brenna folded the kerchief into the pocket of her jacket. They walked silently for a while. "I was missing my younger sister," she said finally.

Camryn nodded. She stopped, took a small picture out of the breast pocket of her green shirt, and handed it to Brenna.

Brenna tried to tilt the glossy photo to see the image in the moonlight. She made out the young girl's face—smiling, a little homely, a little plump, beautiful. Brenna turned the picture over. On the back, in careful printing, were the words "Lauren" and "Twelve."

"This is your sister." Brenna looked up at Cam. "She died with your friend, Dyan?"

"They were murdered." Cam studied the picture over Brenna's shoulder soberly. "Shann thinks they only meant to get Dyan. They wanted to take one Amazon alive, to experiment on, so they took Jess. But Dyan they just wanted to kill. And Lauren...Lauren kind of hero-worshipped Dyan. She followed her around all the time. So she got hit too."

Brenna handed the photo back to Camryn, who returned it carefully to her pocket. They walked on. The rainwashed mountain air was sweet and still.

"So what's your little sister's name?" Camryn asked.

"Samantha. I call her Sam. She's not so little, though. She's going to have a baby."

"Yeah?" Camryn's quick grin held genuine delight.

"Yeah. I'm going to be an aunt."

Brenna allowed her shoulder to brush Cam's arm once as they crested a low rise. They looked at the moonlight shining on the sparse grass at their feet brightly enough to illuminate a pair of shadows they both found familiar. Their shared silence was still silence, but it was easier.

❖

Jess didn't even see Kyla fall. Much as she would curse herself for it later, it wouldn't have mattered if she had.

Kyla's feet shot out from under her so abruptly, she was sliding down the steep, muddy bank before she could even scream.

Jess's immediate whickering whistle snapped Camryn's head up. "Bloody hell," Camryn spat. "Brenna, go east!"

And she was gone. All gangliness fled Cam's body as she flew through the brush at a western angle, in a flexible, cat-like crouch.

"Camryn," Brenna yelled, and then ducked and looked around, furious with herself for the strident noise. "Camryn," she whispered fiercely.

When there was no reply, Brenna hesitated, then ducked into the brush and began her own angle east.

Jess snugged the knot around her waist, yanked the rope to test its hold, and stepped back into open air.

The first drop was only ten feet or so, and the ledge was well padded with mud, but Jess could imagine that, at best, it had knocked the breath from Kyla. Even braced for it and securely roped, her entire abused body jerked when her boots hit the ledge.

The slope itself was so slick with mud, she would be flailing helplessly without the rope to anchor her. Kyla couldn't have hoped to catch herself, or even slow her plummeting slide, for the first hundred yards.

Jess bit back the urge to call out and descended as fast as the wet muck would allow. Her mind was white noise. This was Dyan's blood-sister, Camryn's adonai. *Artemis, guide my hand.*

Jess caught herself halfway down, her scratched hands clenching around the rope. She crouched on her perch, panting, listening with all her strength. She recognized a voice.

❖

Kyla came to rest on her back at the bottom of the muddy hill with her shirt and light jacket racked up almost to her neck and an absolutely miserable wedgie. She stared stupidly up at the blanket of stars above her, her heart pounding in queasy surges.

Her trembling hands moved over her sides. She tried flexing each leg, without any killing pain. She was intact, she decided, just bruised and breathless. Jess would come for her, Kyla was sure of that. Then Camryn would bark her face off. She tried to lie still and let the rest of her wits catch up with her.

The silhouette of a silver-haired woman was haloed against the full moon as she loomed over Kyla, who shrank back instinctively.

"We haven't met, Kyla." The woman's voice was cultured, friendly. "My name is Caster."

❖

"Jesstin?" Caster's amplified voice clanged against the dark hills, jarring the night's silence. "You're aware that one of your little Amazonlettes has joined us, yes?"

There was a pause. Jess waited. And her hands clenched again on the rope, because she knew what was probably happening to Kyla.

Whatever form the pain took—an arm wrenched behind her back or her hair twisted around a fist—Kyla used its energy to broadcast her message with maximum venom. "Fuck this banshee, Jess! Get out of here!"

Jess closed her eyes as a thump sounded. Her knees bent as she felt the blow in her own solar plexus. Jess straightened and made herself focus. She reviewed her options, and then she moved.

❖

Brenna crouched behind a bank of boulders, still shivering with the adrenaline rush, trying to spot Jess somewhere on the hillside in front of her. She couldn't see Kyla among the dense trees at the bottom of the hill, and she couldn't see Cam, who should be coming around the slope across from—

Brenna felt the cool hand slide around her face and clamp over her mouth, and she threw herself backwards, sirens going off in her skull.

Someone caught her thrashing body easily and held her still.

"I don't know you." The musical voice was calm. The hand lifted slightly.

"I'm Brenna," Brenna gasped.

The woman released her. Brenna spun and found herself swimming in a pair of extraordinary gray eyes.

"Hello, Brenna. My name is Shann."

❖

"Of course, I'm no military strategist," Caster told Kyla, "but I assume your compatriots have scattered hither and yon by now, in the surrounding hills?"

"They're digging up our stockpile of machine guns," Kyla panted. She was still breathless from the blow to her stomach, and Dugan and Stuart had to struggle to get her arms and wrists pinned to the grass at Caster's sturdily booted feet.

Kyla assumed the other two orderlies standing watch were Clinic staff. The greasy jerk tying her ankles looked almost spastic with nervousness, but the big guy's greedy gaze on her body chilled her.

"A pity I don't have the manpower for a proper night search in rugged terrain." Caster watched Kyla fight the ropes for a moment. "But perhaps that's fortunate for you, dear, in more ways than one. You'll have only four men to satisfy while we wait for your sisters to join us."

"Five of you, four of us." Kyla tried to snarl, but sweet Gaia, she was scared. "Rifles or not, your odds suck, lady."

"On the contrary, little Amazon, I would say luck has

definitely sided with the interests of science tonight." Caster studied her prisoner. In this moonlight, the girl could be clearly seen from the watching hills. "I'm afraid your matriarchal deities have failed you rather miserably, Kyla. Perhaps you should learn to question goddesses whose benevolence delivers you virtually into the lap of your enemies."

"I'd hold off on gloating, if I were you," Kyla snapped, loathing for this Clinic scientist overcoming her fear. "Jess is not just going to come strolling in here—"

"Of course she is, dear, and we both know it." Caster smiled. "I knew once I had one of you, recapturing the others would be fairly straightforward. You're bait, little Kyla. You'll help me reel the others in. I finally have a use for this adanin-fixation you Amazons share." She reached for the girl's soft hair again and narrowly missed having her fingers bitten off.

"In some ways you're not unlike that coarse medic you've befriended, girl. She, too, snapped at the hand that fed her. She's no Amazon, of course." Caster's voice grew flinty. "Brenna is a traitorous little sheep led about by her vapid young vulva."

Jesstin, Kyla thought. *Please, adanin, run.*

❖

Jess knew two things as the rope ran out and she sidestepped freestyle down the slope. She knew Caster would hurt Kyla if she didn't surrender as ordered. And she knew that together, she and Kyla had to buy Cam and Brenna time to maneuver.

Jess straightened at the base of the hill and caught her breath. She held her arms slightly away from her sides as the two men on watch spotted her and yelled, snapping their rifles up to cover her.

Kyla moaned and turned her head in the grass when she saw Jess emerge from the trees.

Jess's eyes went flat when she saw Kyla's body, helplessly spread beneath the eyes of several men. She stopped at the entrance to the enclosure.

Then Caster nodded at Stuart, and the carefully scripted capture began.

It didn't go at all as Caster intended. Stuart was supposed to start stripping the girl on the ground, for one thing. Ripping her shirt open would surely cause Jesstin to make a rash move, but the cretin chose that crucial moment to go clumsy. He knelt and fumbled with Kyla's shirt, his hands shaking.

Caster had wanted Dugan to do the stripping, but the burly guard had refused in favor of subduing Jesstin. Some macho resentment of her Amazonian prowess, apparently. He and the two other orderlies waited until Jess broke and dived for Kyla, which was the second thing that went wrong. They should have moved much sooner.

Jess broke Stuart's neck with her heel as she flew over Kyla's pinned body, then flipped once in a tight arc. She landed well but staggered, the ache in her lower back sudden and immense. The injury she'd received days ago in the Clinic's arena awoke with a snarling burst of pain.

Kyla yelled, pistoning her knees as much as the ropes would allow, trying to shift Stuart's slumping bulk off of her as Dugan and the others finally took Jess down.

Caster picked up the megaphone again and crouched beside Kyla. She wrapped her hand around the girl's throat and held her as the men beat Jess. After a minute or so, Caster raised the megaphone. "Camryn, dear? Are you watching?"

❖

Brenna was never clear how they found Camryn. She concentrated on following Shann's cloaked figure, dodging slapping branches as they twisted through trees and skirting exposed areas of rock as they moved steadily west. When Caster's call reached them, Brenna froze in place, her mind going blank with shock.

"You know that voice?" Shann was short of breath, but her words were low and calm.

Brenna managed to nod. "It's Caster. She's a scientist at the Clinic. She heads the Tristaine study."

"All right, tell me more later." Shann's warm hand clasped Brenna's arm. She noticed the intertwining lines of color adorning the older woman's wrist as she adjusted the heavy pack she carried. Then Shann looked up sharply, and at the same moment, Brenna heard the snapping of brush ahead of them.

Camryn was running blind, covering ground in great ragged leaps. She raced through the trees to their left, and even Shann's low, urgent whistle didn't slow her down.

"Brenna, stop her!"

Brenna was running before Shann's words were out, and unlike her quarry, she wasn't weakened by Prison field work and poor rations. She caught Camryn after a rough sprint and snatched the back of her shirt, but when she twisted free, Brenna simply threw herself at her.

Camryn's flailing elbow punched into Brenna's stomach, and breath gushed out of her lungs as they rolled on the marshy ground. Somehow she managed to hold on to the thrashing girl.

When Shann reached them, she laid a hand on Camryn's back. "Be still, little sister."

Brenna felt the wave of recognition move through Cam's body, and she let go of her in stages, both of them gasping for breath.

"Shann." Cam got to her knees and grabbed Shann's hands. "Lady, it's a City patrol. They have Jesstin and Kyla."

"I feared as much." Shann knelt, too, and looked up into Cam's face. "Are you all right, Camryn?"

"Yeah, and so is Ky, but Jesstin's taken some bad hits. Shann, we have to move!"

"Not yet, adanin. We can't help them by racing into an open trap."

To Brenna's astonishment, Camryn made no attempt to refute her leader. She stared at Shann mutely and then sat slowly back on her heels, still pulling for breath.

Shann motioned Brenna closer, and their small circle closed, shutting out the suddenly menacing darkness.

Camryn peered over Shann's shoulder. "Where are the others, lady?"

"I've come alone."

"What?"

"I have much to tell you, and more to ask. Let's find a base to monitor Caster's camp and then hold council." Shann's tone gentled. "Take a moment and rest with me, little sister. I haven't seen your face in far too long."

Some of the fierceness drained out of Camryn's body, and she sighed. She surprised Brenna a second time by leaning into Shann and resting her head in her lap, then wrapping her wiry arms around her waist. Shann stroked her back and kept a careful watch on the silent hill.

For a moment, Brenna had an irrational desire to take Cam's place. Jess's absence was an aching void in her heart, and her hands were cold with fear.

They were in position an hour later and ready by sunrise.

❖

Dawn.

Jess hadn't been sure she'd live to see it, and she wasn't sure she appreciated having done so. She stood, after a fashion, close to Kyla, her wrists tied tightly between two trees. Even when her knees buckled, as they did frequently, the pull on her arms kept her stiffly erect.

The savage beating had continued until Jess passed out. Her kidneys were still intact, she thought, feeling the first warm rays of the sun touch her battered face. No bones were broken, but she was probably a sight to frighten young children. When they'd strung her up, Kyla had wept just seeing her face by firelight.

"Jesstin?"

Jess heard the anxiety and exhaustion in her younger

sister's voice, and she forced her eyes open again. She and Kyla had talked in the last hours, briefly and quietly, whenever Jess was conscious.

"How are you doing?" Worry was obviously winning over weariness.

"I'm upright," Jess croaked.

"Jess." Kyla was silent for a moment. "She'd get rid of Brenna, wouldn't she?"

"What?"

"I've been thinking." Still lying staked to the dew-soaked grass, Kyla was shivering, and not entirely from cold. "I know this fancy doctor bitch wants the three of us back. But she wouldn't have any use for Brenna. Right? If Brenna's captured too, would she—?"

"Probably."

The "p" sound hurt her split lip. Jess didn't think Caster would have much use for her, either, if she had Camryn. All the Clinic needed was a new matched pair to resume the study with the current protocol, but Kyla didn't need to know that yet.

"What would we do, you and me?" Kyla's voice was soft. "If it were Cam and Brenna here, and us out there? I've been trying to imagine what Dyan would say. What would she tell us to—"

"Not this," Jess hissed, and she straightened abruptly.

Kyla turned her head on the grass to see Brenna, in full view, stepping out of the trees and into the camp.

❖

Given a choice between vomiting and her knees giving out, Brenna thought she would rather not throw up. She hoped neither would happen, and she'd just keep making her way over the uneven grass toward Jess and Kyla until someone spotted her.

She caught Jess's eye and quickly learned that was a mistake, so she concentrated on Kyla instead. An unexpected burst of anger swept Brenna when she saw Kyla's convulsive shivering. She spotted a folded blanket abandoned on the grass nearby and made a side trip to pick it up.

She took the opportunity to survey the rest of Caster's camp behind the two captives. Three pup tents, stacks of supplies. Nothing human stirred. Then she saw an orderly, a bearded face she vaguely remembered from the Clinic, rifle folded in his arms, supposedly keeping watch, but he wasn't looking toward them.

Brenna knelt beside Kyla in the wet grass.

"What the bloody hell do you think you're doing?" Kyla growled.

Brenna put a calming hand on the girl's side. She could feel Jess's glare burning a hole in the top of her head. "Drawing attention. If the damn guard ever wakes up."

She shook the army blanket out and spread it over Kyla. "Did they hurt you, Ky?"

Kyla's eyes closed as Brenna's hands smoothed the soft warmth around her. "You better have a bomb taped to your chest."

"Answer me, Kyla. Are you injured?"

"I'm fine. Just shook. You mother me worse than Shann. You better look at Jess." Kyla shivered again. "You and Cam do have some kind of plan, right?"

Brenna glanced up at Jess. "As a matter of fact, Shann's here. She had to come alone, but she's—"

"About bloody time," Jess snapped above them. She kept her voice low and craned her neck painfully to see the arena around them.

"You knew she was coming?" Kyla's eyes narrowed dangerously. "Do you think you might have mentioned that, Jesstin, some time in the last two days?"

"No, I didn't know Shann was coming, but it makes sense," Jess replied. "It's what Dyan would do."

Still no movement anywhere in the camp. The orderly on

watch actually seemed to be dozing. The corner of Jess's mouth lifted mirthlessly. Caster's goons wouldn't last ten seconds against Amazons if it weren't for the rifles.

Brenna made herself stand and face Jess. She looked fully into her bruised face. "Well, I knew you'd look something like this," she said, and then burst into tears, which startled them both.

"Get a grip, Bren," Jess said quietly.

"I am." Brenna shook her head once. "It's just nerves. I told you that." She rested her hands on Jess's sides, blinking until she could see again.

"Turn so I block the guard's view," Jess whispered, but Brenna shook her head.

"No, he's supposed to see me," Brenna said, wincing at the tightness of the rope cutting into Jess's wrists. "Shann wants a general shift of attention toward this side of the camp, around us."

"How are you with knots?"

"Slow down." Brenna opened Jess's black shirt, which was hanging in dusty tatters. "This is as close as I'll ever come to having you tied up and at my mercy again, Jesstin, so I'm going to take advantage of it while I can."

"Brenna—"

"There's nothing we can do until Shann and Camryn move, Jess. Stop snarling at me and let me look at you."

"Yep, she's Shann all over again," Kyla observed from the grass.

Jess sighed as Brenna curled her hands around her back. Great, she thought. Brenna would probably probe areas that were so tender Jess might yell out loud, in front of Kyla.

Brenna numbly closed Jess's shirt. Last night's damage, added to the punishment she'd already taken, made her wonder how Jess was conscious at all.

Brenna looked up into her eyes again, and again. That was

their mutual undoing. Jess's stern gaze softened, and Brenna released a long breath and sank against her. She slid her arms around Jess's waist and rested her forehead carefully against the hard swell of her shoulder.

"Do you realize we've had the worst fucking courtship in history?" Brenna asked finally.

Jess arched an eyebrow and Kyla chuckled. "Bren...adanin. I'm afraid we don't have time for—"

"It's going to be our last chance, for a while." Brenna sniffed and lifted her head. "Camryn and Shann will kick it off pretty soon. Kyla, both of you, just be ready."

"And just what are they kicking?" Jess asked hollowly. "Two unarmed Amazons against three men, five rifles, and one mad-banshee scientist?"

"Shann says to remember Dyan's last training." Brenna lifted her brows, hoping this made sense. "She told me to remind you that Dyan's last order was still in stock."

"In stock?" Kyla looked puzzled. "You mean in effect?"

"No, in stock," Jess said, suddenly looking healthier than she had moments before. "Not Dyan's last order, the last ordnance in stock. The last supplies she ordered."

Brenna nodded.

"Of what, already?" Kyla pleaded.

"It was a training in explosives, Ky, remember?" Jess explained. "Shann brought dyna—"

That's when the other end of the camp blew up.

CHAPTER NINE

The sudden blast shattered the dawn stillness, and even Brenna, who'd been braced for it, started hard and gripped Jess's waist with icy fingers. It was only two sticks, thrown from strategic positions above Caster's camp, but in the sleeping silence their sharp concussion carried as much shock value as an A-bomb.

The orderly assigned to sentry duty came awake with a startled yell, firing twice into the air before he was fully on his feet. That's all Brenna saw before she focused on freeing Jess and Kyla.

She had, in fact, sequestered something in the most convenient hiding place available, her cleavage. Not a bomb, but a small utility knife. Jess's eyes widened a little when Brenna retrieved it, but she seemed to appreciate the blade's efficiency in cutting through the ropes holding her erect.

Brenna helped Kyla stand, and the two of them were able to support Jess, but they were a swaying, clutching group for the first disorienting moments of the fight.

There was shouting now, male voices as well as Amazon war cries, and the dirt thrown by the TNT thickened the mountain air, transforming the enclosed camp into a hazy battlefield. The dynamite itself had not injured anyone, and Brenna guessed Shann and Camryn had placed it carefully with that intent. Amazons tried not to kill unless necessary, the guiding premise of Tristaine's warrior women, according to Shann.

Caster's orderlies put up a respectable fight once roused. Any resolve to preserve the lives of potential study subjects quickly dissolved. Tent flaps opened, and dark muzzles emerged to spit barks of thunder and snaps of red fire through the haze.

Jess had one arm around Brenna's neck and the other around Kyla's. The strength was returning to her legs, and walking was possible now. They were headed back toward the trees Brenna had emerged from only minutes before, but Jess hesitated, craning her head back to assess the fight behind them. She stopped abruptly and lifted her arms from the shoulders of the smaller women.

"Go on," Jess said.

"Hey!" Brenna caught Jess's hand. "Shann said to wait for her at the top of—"

"Good idea," Jess said, still trying to see her other sisters through the dust and confusion of running bodies, shouts, and rifle fire. She pulled her hand from Brenna's grip. "See you there."

"Jesstin, you are not—"

But Jess was gone, moving stiffly but gaining speed as she disappeared into the hanging cloud of dust enveloping the camp.

"Brenna?" Kyla touched Brenna's shoulder. "You might need to understand Jesstin a little better. Amazons can't just—"

"Kyla," Brenna interrupted, "maybe you, and Jess, and every other Amazon in punching distance needs to start understanding *me* a little better!"

And she was gone too, yelling curses at Jess. Kyla threw a look to the heavens and followed her sisters into battle.

Without the unlamented Stuart, Caster's forces consisted of Dugan, two other men, and five rifles. Brenna coughed and squinted in time to catch a fleeting impression of the status of the clash.

Shann was stronger than her slenderness implied, but she struggled with an orderly easily twice her size. She used his bulk against him to good effect, but she was no warrior, and the rifle clenched between the combatants could still be won by either.

Brenna's stomach gave a nasty clench when she saw Jess

tackle the burly man who grappled with Shann, but her attention was riveted by Caster standing ten yards to her right, swinging up a rifle at some target behind her and taking careful aim.

Brenna started for the scientist before the rifle discharged, knowing only that the bullet was intended for an Amazon. She heard a cry of pain—Kyla, Camryn, she wasn't sure who'd been hit—and then she leaped on Caster, hard enough to knock them both breathless, and carried her to the ground. The rifle flew from Caster's hands as she fell, and she gave an unladylike grunt as her body smacked the earth.

Brenna rolled with her, filling with a bone-deep fury she should have expected, with the Clinic incarnate flailing beneath her. Then she chanced a look toward the far tents and froze in dismay.

Camryn lay curled on her side in the grass, clutching her lower leg, her face locked in a grimace of pain. Kyla crouched over her, her own features pale as chalk, scanning the arena for any new threat. The second orderly lay sprawled unconscious on the grass nearby. One of the young Amazons must have dropped him before Cam was felled by Caster's bullet. That still left Dugan.

Caster flung a handful of dirt and grass into Brenna's face like a veteran of such cowardly ploys, and Brenna instinctively ground her fists into her eyes to clear them. Caster had just enough time to club Brenna soundly in the stomach with her fists, and then Dugan was on them, wrenching Brenna up off the gasping Caster.

"Hey! Hey, Brenna!" Dugan roared. "Don't you fight me now, pretty lady." He pinned Brenna's arms to her sides and pressed her against his chest, dancing to avoid her vicious kicks.

Vicious, but not random. Brenna knew human anatomy well, and she'd been kickboxing long enough to aim for truly vulnerable areas. Brenna didn't connect squarely. Her gouging knee only sideswept Dugan's crotch, but it was enough to make him stagger and bellow with surprise.

But not enough to release her. Instead, Dugan dropped where he stood, pulling Brenna down with him, until he straddled her supine body in the grass, one knee on either side of her. His face was distorted with both rage and pain, and he slapped her, hard. Brenna groped for the exquisitely tender soft spots between the jaw and the ear, but Dugan trapped her wrists in one hand and flattened himself over her.

"I told you to try to be friendlier," he breathed in Brenna's ear as she struggled beneath him. "Parading down the hall by me a dozen times a day."

Jesstin's boot rocketed into Dugan's ribs, knocking him off Brenna and onto his side. She lifted herself on her hands and skittered backwards, clawing the grass to put distance between them.

Brenna stared up at Jess, appalled. She had finally reached the end of her formidable strength. The powerful kick had apparently drained the last of Jess's energy, and she crumpled when Dugan grabbed her legs.

Dugan pulled Jess down beneath him and fastened his hairy hands around her throat. He hissed at her and his spittle hit her cheek, but Jess couldn't even turn her head to avoid it. She had little hope of breaking his pinkie fingers, and no hope whatever of dislodging his weight. She saw Dugan's broad shoulders above her, and the sunlight outlining them began to darken to red in her vision as his large hands choked off her breathing.

Vaguely, Jess heard Brenna cry out somewhere close by, and Kyla scream Shann's name. Then nothing for a few seconds, except pressure and pain and the desperate hunger for air. Jess's senses had started to fade when she heard the muted crack from Shann's rifle.

The big man stiffened over Jess, his hands jerking away from her throat. Gasping, Jess made a huge effort and managed to twist out from under Dugan before he fell, his skull shattered. She came to rest on her back, staring up at the morning sky brightening through the smoke and dust, and then both sound and light faded.

❖

When her vision cleared, Jess was lying with her head pillowed in Brenna's soft lap. Her head pounded sickly, only the most insistent of the aches awaiting her return to awareness, but fear filled her more urgently than pain.

"Where's Shann?" Jess began to sit up, but Brenna gently pressed her shoulders flat.

"Shann's all right, Jess." Brenna's teeth were chattering as if she were freezing. "Kyla is too. So am I. Camryn…Cam's been shot, but it's superficial."

A muffled exclamation escaped Jess and she tried to sit up again, but only until the pounding in her head hit a huge bass note.

"Jesstin, lie still!" Brenna pushed her back down, too easily, her own eyes filling with tears she was too distracted to notice. "It's over. We're okay! Shann's got them covered. Don't sit up. Just look there."

Brenna supported Jess's head so she could focus on the odd tableau at the other end of the camp. Shann, looking dusty and disheveled, but reasonably composed, was holding one of the rifles on the only orderly still functional enough to walk. He had just finished dumping the last of three male bodies into the Clinic jeep—one unconscious, two corpses—and now, under Shann's silent gaze, he was escorting Caster to the waiting vehicle.

Caster was limping, her clothing was torn, and she didn't spare Brenna or Jess a glance. She paused as she reached Shann, and the two women regarded each other for a long moment.

"It's a pity we have no historians present to record this auspicious moment, Shann of Tristaine." Caster's rasping words reached them faintly. "The meeting of two great adversaries—the leader of a doomed band of renegade women and the scientist who will one day preside over her dissection."

"We might meet again, Caster." They had to strain to hear Shann's low voice. "But the women of Tristaine will thrive for centuries after we're both dust."

"Poetic, your highness, but delusional." Caster's bitter gaze moved past the silent Amazon and focused on Jess and Brenna. "You'll see me again too, ladies," she called. "Brenna, I've found a lovely slave camp for you in one of the outer boroughs. You'll help me mount Jesstin's head over my mantle, dear, before I have you branded and shipped."

Then Caster lifted herself into the front of the jeep, her clothing tattered, a bleeding scratch on her throat, and her hair a snarled cap around her head, but her poise fully restored. She folded her hands serenely in her lap while the orderly keyed the ignition.

Shann kept the rifle trained on the hulking black transport as it lumbered out of the camp and down a dry riverbed toward the base of the foothills. She waited until the sound of its powerful engine faded, then rested the empty rifle against a stump. "Brenna? Do you need me?"

"We're all right, Shann," Brenna called. Their voices sounded unnaturally loud in the renewed stillness of the mountain air. "Jess is stable for now. See about Camryn."

Shann nodded and went to Cam, who sat with her back against a tree as Kyla bound her bleeding leg.

Jess shifted in Brenna's arms and lifted herself on one elbow. "Hey!" Jess barked at Camryn, almost accusingly.

"She'll be okay, Jesstin," Kyla called over her shoulder, never taking her eyes from her work. Shann knelt beside her and checked her younger sister for signs of shock, taking her pulse, feeling her hands.

"I got shot," Camryn informed Jess. She sounded surprised, and she was ashen, but she didn't seem particularly dismayed.

"You should have ducked," Jess snapped.

"Jess, she had a rifle," Camryn protested.

"You should have ducked," Shann and Jess said together,

and Kyla snorted laughter and hugged Shann, though she herself was crying, now that they were safe.

Jess rolled back into Brenna's lap with a muffled groan. "Dyan's response to every injury in the ranks," she explained to Brenna.

"Thank you. I wondered." Brenna smiled. Her pulse was slowing to a bearable cadence again, and she cradled Jess's face in her hands. "Jesstin, when you stand up, how many parts of you are going to drop off?"

"I hope my head does." Jess shivered once, hard.

"Shann, can you bring us a—" Brenna stopped speaking as she looked up to see Shann kneeling beside them, already snapping out an army blanket. "Thanks," she said instead, and helped Shann tuck it around Jess's shaking body.

"How good are you at extracting bullets?" Shann asked Brenna quietly.

"I've done it on corpses." Brenna swallowed. "But I know we don't have the right instruments. All we have is a first aid kit. I don't suppose there's any way we could get Cam down to the City?" Her voice trailed off. She didn't need either of the Amazons to answer that. "Shann, please tell me you packed antibiotics as well as dynamite."

"Some." Shann nodded. "I did bring medical supplies, and I've seen some herbs we can use nearby."

"Herbs," Brenna repeated politely.

Shann smiled down at Jess, who was gazing at her blearily. "Hello, Jesstin." She leaned over and rested her lips against Jess's forehead for a long moment, then straightened. "I'll wait until Brenna gets you back on your feet, adanin, and then I intend to knock you senseless myself."

"Hey, I did everything right." Jess was puzzled. The warmth of the blanket and their hands was reaching her now, and she was able to relax a bit. "We had to move earlier than we thought, but we got everyone out." Her expressive brows furrowed. "You mean the route? The path we took through the foothills? Shann, that was the shortest, easiest way. It was dumb luck that Caster—"

"I mean drop-kicking a two hundred-pound man hours after a bad beating," Shann interrupted calmly. "The latest in a series of them, from the looks of you. How is she, Brenna?"

"Not good." Brenna brushed Jess's hair back. She was measuring her warmth, but she also wanted Jess to feel her touch. "She's got a nasty fever that comes and goes, and it's rising again. I haven't had a chance to examine her thoroughly, but I don't think anything's broken. There's no sign of internal bleeding, but she's exhausted, just worn out."

Jess thought of refuting this clinical assessment, but she was too tired to care. Brenna's lap was too soft and the blanket too warm. She heard Shann's worried voice faintly, far above her.

"Is she unconscious?"

"Asleep." Brenna's smile was evident in her tone. "Listen."

Jess was snoring softly, secure in the certainty that her sisters were safe.

❖

They had the rifles, and they had the dry riverbank. Both advantages allowed them to take over Caster's abandoned camp temporarily, rather than drag their injured sisters farther into the hills. A view of the riverbed below would give them a little warning if Clinic forces returned, and the rifles would provide a quick defense if needed.

Brenna helped Jess as far as an old stump near the tents, where they were setting up a makeshift infirmary. Jess rested her tender back carefully against the gnarled wood and waited until Camryn settled on the grass in front of her.

"You're all right with this?" Jess asked Camryn quietly. "I trust Brenna's skill, Cam, but this is the first time you've taken a strike in battle. You know you can ask for Shann."

"'Sokay." Camryn's face was ashen as Kyla helped her ease back into Jess's arms. "If that blondie can dig thorns out of Kyla without a lot of screaming, this'll be a cinch."

Jess rested her chin in Camryn's hair and returned Kyla's wan smile. She pressed her younger sister's freckled shoulders once in thanks.

"Even if Cam didn't need to be restrained for this, she'd want Jess to brace her." Shann helped Brenna carry their assembled supplies to the stump. "Camryn and Jesstin are the only two warriors among us. If an Amazon is injured in battle, she often chooses a warrior to see her through the first healing, so she can absorb her strength."

"What strength?" Kyla asked flatly. "Jess is worse off than Cam, if you're going by total of bruises." She crouched beside Jess and touched the back of her neck, trying to get her to finish the last of Shann's herbal tea. Cam had already downed two cups, and her eyes were a bit glassy.

"Dang, why do you guys all have such cold hands," Jess complained, swallowing the tea with a grimace.

"I'm nervous." Kyla showed Jess her trembling fingers. "Excuse me, I've never seen a bullet get cut out of my lover's leg before. Oops." She bit her lip.

They all looked at Shann, who continued laying out medical supplies, unruffled.

"You're such a wimp, Ky." Leaning back against Jess, trying to be tough and more than a little high, Camryn snickered. "My hands aren't cold. I bet Shann's hands aren't cold either, and I know Jess's aren't—"

Cam squeaked as Shann brushed her thin wrist with icy fingers.

"I'm nervous too." Shann smiled, which transformed her briefly from a handsome woman into a beautiful one. "I've seen this done, far too many times, but it's always hard to witness a sister's suffering." She nodded at Brenna, who was kneeling beside her. "Luckily, the one adanin among us who must be cool is steady as a rock. Are we ready, Blades?"

"That's your second name now," Kyla warned Brenna. "Once Shann dubs you, you're dubbed for life."

"Well, I'm glad I was cutting when Shann dubbed me, instead of doing a rectal."

Camryn tittered, and Jess dropped Brenna a grateful wink.

Brenna flattened her hands on her lap for a moment, and her gaze grew hazy as she concentrated, picturing the procedure. Cam was a patient now, and her patients got her best efforts. In spite of the quivering in her stomach, Brenna's hands on her thighs were steady and warm. She drew on thin rubber gloves from the medical kit and smiled at the pale Amazon who reclined in Jess's arms. "Guess I'm ready, if my victim is."

"Wait." Cam scowled. "I'm probably going to yell. Just so you know, and don't freak when it happens."

"Beware Amazon macha, Camryn." Jess smiled at Brenna over Cam's shoulder. "Remember Dyan and the rosebush. Scream your bloody head off if you want."

"Okay." Cam smiled agreeably at Kyla as she knelt beside her and took her hand.

It was a grueling twenty minutes for all of them.

Brenna had been right. It was a superficial wound, if any such trauma to human tissue can be termed superficial. The small-caliber bullet had penetrated the large muscle of Camryn's left calf. Brenna understood healing at an instinctive level, so the procedure was largely common sense. But she was using rudimentary instruments, sterilized in boiling water and alcohol, and the work was harrowing and slow. Camryn was quickly coated with sweat, in spite of the late-morning chill, and so was her healer.

Cam cried out twice, and each time Jess's arms tightened in comfort, as Shann braced her leg. Later, Camryn would claim that her worst suffering came from Kyla crushing her fingers the second time she yelled.

Only Shann and Brenna watched the extraction directly, both with rapt fascination. They worked together like a team long familiar with each other's skills, Shann handing Brenna instruments and monitoring Camryn's breathing and pulse. But Brenna was never unaware of the pain Cam was feeling. She gave them both breathers twice that Cam denied needing.

Kyla was paler than the patient by the time Brenna patted a sterile cloth over Cam's leg to dry it before bandaging. Cam let out a long breath of relief, and her eyes drifted shut as she rested her head on Jess's shoulder. Jess looked as spent as she did.

Shann eyed her sisters with pragmatic sympathy. "Are you going to faint, Kyla?"

"Oh, no." Kyla's voice shook as she played with Cam's hand. "I'll be fine, lady. I always look like this when bullets get cut out of my lover's leg. It's just nerves."

Then she burst into tears, and Brenna and Jess exchanged weary smiles.

❖

"I'm a felon," Brenna murmured.

She didn't realize she'd spoken aloud until she felt Shann's hand on her shoulder. She started and sat up, and smiled at her self-consciously. "Sorry. I think I'm beginning to hallucinate."

"It's no wonder." Shann's rich voice was kind. "You're exhausted, Blades. Why don't you sleep for a while? I can finish this."

"Aye, why don't both of you sleep for a while?" Jess growled. "I'm as clean as I'm going to get, thanks."

Jess was referring to the alcohol bath Brenna had bared her to the waist to receive an hour before. She had taken Camryn's place on the pallet beneath the huge tree when her fever rose to the point that she couldn't hold a coherent conversation. The mild summer weather made it possible for them to forego Caster's musty tents, and sleeping under stars was always the preference in Tristaine.

Camryn and Kyla lay on a blanketed air mattress nearby, talking quietly. The wide bandage on Camryn's leg glowed a ghostly white by the light of the small fire that crackled warmly in the center of their circle.

It was late, after midnight. Brenna had left her wristwatch somewhere under Dugan, and she missed the sense of order that knowing the time might have provided. As happened frequently now, when Brenna felt unsettled, she looked at Jess. This time, it didn't bring the reassurance she'd hoped for. She was lying half-propped against the tree, still shaking with fever, even after a long, cooling bath. Brenna felt bleak with worry.

"I'd make you suck on a thermostrip again," she said, touching Jess's face, "but knowing the exact reading wouldn't change much. I can tell it's as high as it was an hour ago."

Kyla lifted her head from Camryn's shoulder. "Did you give her the teasel, Shann?"

"It was in the tea." Shann fastened Jess's shirt, then rested her hand on her warrior's side. "That should help cool the fever, Jesstin. You'll be on your feet again tomorrow, but there'll be no traveling for a few days. You and Camryn both need time to recover. I've rarely seen such a daunting collection of dents and bruises."

"We should have ducked, Jess," Camryn said sadly.

"I know," Jess sighed.

"But we'll not want to spend any more time in the lowlands than absolutely necessary." Shann surveyed the tents, and the small craters made in the dusty ground from dynamite blasts. "Once we're able to travel, we can set up a base camp in the lower range beyond the next valley. There's fish and game there to feed us, and it's far enough from City eyes to be safe."

"Well, you two better heal fast." Kyla yawned, rubbing her cheek on Camryn's breast. "We can only camp out down here, eating snared rabbits, for two weeks. We have to be home before the Festival of Thesmophoria. The thought of drowning out that lousy, lame little soprano Deidre in the midsummer music festival is what kept me from braining a Prison guard with a pot down there. The Festival's great, Brenna. There are footraces, dances, a big feast."

"And Kyla has the most beautiful voice in Tristaine." Cam spoke with unabashed pride. "The artists' guild snapped her up when she was ten."

"Adanin." Shann's low voice was kind. "We can't go home. Not yet."

Brenna glanced at Jess. She lay still beneath the thin blanket, but her feverish eyes closed for a moment.

"Huh?" Camryn sat up, supported by Kyla's arm. "How long is yet?"

"For several weeks, at least. The three of you are convicted felons, Camryn. City agents can legally enter Tristaine to search for us." Shann's voice was as gentle as ever, but Brenna was beginning to sense the aura of command that made her a leader of Amazons. "Our best chance is to lose ourselves in this maze of foothills and avoid their patrols."

"Lady, we can't hide from the City forever." Cam's tone was respectful, but color was filling her sallow cheeks. "They're gonna come after us, but that's why we need to go home, Shann. It's not just us they want, it's Tristaine."

Kyla put a quieting hand on Camryn's side.

"It's all right, Kyla." There was pride in Shann's smile. "Dyan chose Camryn for Tristaine's council for both her intelligence and her candor. But, Kyla, you're troubled too, little sister. What are your thoughts?"

"I think that without Dyan, and you, and Jesstin, and Cam, our council's going to be divided." Kyla's brow looked creased with worry. "But even if everyone agrees on how to handle the City, Tristaine looks to you for guidance, lady. Our sisters need you now, more than ever."

"And when Caster nails a warrant for Shann's arrest to the door of Tristaine's main lodge, Kyla?" Jess's soft burr drew their eyes to her. "Will our sisters turn her over without a fight? Will they give any of us over to the City?"

"So we'll fight." The muscles stood out in Camryn's jaw. "It's going to come to that anyway, Jesstin."

"If it comes to that, adanin, Tristaine is lost." Jess fixed the young warrior with her eyes. "Dyan knew that. We all know it."

"Brenna, this affects you too."

Brenna started when Shann rested her hand on her knee.

"You know our enemies well, and if you stay with us, your fate will be joined with Tristaine's. Your word carries weight in this council, Blades, so speak your heart."

Brenna glanced at Jess. "Well…I think we have time. Caster wants to avoid war too, for her own reasons. This Clinic study was supposed to discover some other way of defeating Tristaine, and we got out before it was finished."

"We" has changed again, Brenna thought. *Jess, me, and now these three Amazons. "We" is becoming Tristaine.*

"So, for a while anyway," she concluded, "Caster has nothing to offer the Military. And there's got to be all kinds of uproar about our escape. The Clinic will have to do a lot of fast talking to keep the contract." Brenna made herself meet Shann's measuring look. "I think it's safe to wait. It'll be some time before the City can move."

"I'm not saying we're banished forever, sisters." Shann looked at Camryn and Kyla. "But long enough to make it seem feasible that we've fled the County. We can go home when the City's grip on the mountains eases and we can slip past their patrols."

Camryn dropped her eyes and nodded.

"I can't believe Deidre gets to sing my solo." Kyla sighed and rested her head on Camryn's shoulder again. "All right, Shann."

"Thank you, adanin. And now, for our wounded, sleep will help more than anything else. I've never had much success at giving you direct orders, Jesstin, but I want you to obey a friendly request, all right? Lie still for a few hours."

"Sure," Jess mumbled.

"A friendly request." Brenna smiled, pulling the blanket up over Jess's chest. "That works with Amazons?"

"Sometimes," Shann said. "Even Jess." She rose gracefully to her feet and fed a few small branches to their dancing fire.

Camryn and Kyla lay down together, and soon their quiet murmurings drifted into silence.

Brenna measured Jess's fever with her hand, then took her pulse. She was resting comfortably enough. Brenna was tired, but too wired to possibly find sleep.

"You must be in severe culture shock."

Brenna blinked as Shann settled beside her again. "Me?"

Shann gathered her legs beneath her and leaned back on one hand to study Brenna. "Let me see if I understand what's happened to you. You were a reasonably successful Government medic. You were assigned to Jesstin's project, what, less than a month ago?"

Brenna nodded.

"So, in a few weeks, you've had your faith in your leaders dashed, you've lost your home and your career and any sense of security. And now you're running for your life through a mountain wilderness with four strange women, one of whom you've fallen in love with, while people are blowing things up and trying to kill you." Shann lifted an eyebrow and for a moment resembled Jess. "Is that about right?"

Brenna smiled. "I think you covered it."

"You must feel like you've fallen in with some bizarre cult."

Brenna winced. "Well, no, I hadn't thought of that one, thanks."

Shann laughed again and then covered her mouth when Jess stirred between them.

Brenna tucked the blanket around Jess's long legs. "Shann?"

"Yes, Blades."

"I don't know how you feel about me being here." She smoothed Jess's hair off her forehead. "Jess asked me to come, but the rest of you weren't counting on an extra body." She hesitated. "A body that was on the other side, herself, only a month ago. I don't know why any of you should trust me. I'm an outsider, basically."

"You probably always have been, basically." Shann shrugged. "That's why most women seek out Tristaine. They come to us because they don't belong in the City."

"That's what Jess said." Brenna considered this statement silently for a while. She could have refuted the idea that she'd willingly sought out anything except an honest paycheck in the beginning, but she wasn't even sure that was true anymore.

"Tristaine isn't unique, Blades." Shann brushed a pine needle off Jess's arm. "At least we don't think we are, communication between Counties being what it is. We believe there might be one or two clans very like Tristaine for every City in the Nation. Full of people who don't fit in."

"That's what the City tabloids say," Brenna said carefully.

Shann grinned at her. "Adanin, take your time. If you ever feel you must leave us, we'll find a way to get you somewhere safe. Just let things happen at their own pace for now."

"I'm trying." Brenna cleared her throat. "I guess this is as good a time as any to draw a clean slate, wherever I end up. It's not like I'm leaving a lot behind. Except for my sister, I have no family. I've always been good at my work, though."

Shann nodded. "I wouldn't have let you take the bullet from Cam's leg if I didn't believe that. I'd have done it myself."

Brenna lifted an eyebrow. "You've done surgical procedures? I thought you worked more with vitamins and plants."

"I use natural remedies, but a healer among warrior women gets far too much practice sewing her sisters back together." Shann's eyes were warm. "I asked you to help Cam because I wanted the others to know you have my trust."

"Shann, you just met me."

"Jesstin trusts you." Shann's long fingers stroked the warrior's arm. "A woman capable of claiming this Amazon's heart is worthy of our respect. You care very much for her, don't you?"

Brenna stared at Jess's still face, and she felt a sense of wonder. "Yes, I do. I've never…this is the first…" She gestured helplessly, searching for words. "And now it's not just Jess, it's the rest of you, too. I've never had friends…well, you're becoming friends…" She trailed off.

"I often wish we hadn't lost so much of our grandmothers' language." Shann brushed a lock of hair off Brenna's forehead, and she felt a warm shiver. "Today, we only have remnants. We struggle with such paltry, inadequate terms for friendship, but the early Amazons had many ways of describing the bonds between women. I think I understand what you're saying, Brenna. We're becoming your adanin, too, right?"

"Right." Brenna slumped in relief. "Thanks."

They both looked down at Jess, who was tightening beneath the blanket, her brow growing tense.

Brenna shifted closer to her and slipped her hand beneath Jess's hair to cup the back of her neck. "This helps her relax, sometimes." Brenna kneaded the tight muscles at the base of Jess's skull.

"Good. I used that touch to ease Dyan's headaches, the ones my herbs couldn't help."

Brenna looked up at the touch of sadness in Shann's voice.

"Did you know Dyan was my wife? I don't know how much Jess told you about her sisters."

"No. I knew you and Dyan were on Tristaine's council, but not that you were bonded, Shann. I'm sorry."

"Thank you, Brenna. I'm sorry, too. I wish you could have known Dyan." Shann's eyes shimmered in the firelight. "She'd snarl to hear us called 'bonded,' though. Another of those new

Tristainian terms. Dyan was my wife, and I was hers. In the old language, the word 'wife' is a prayer, in and of itself. I've always liked that."

Brenna smiled. "I like that, too."

Shann looked down at Jess, who had relaxed again in the grass. "Why don't you stretch out for a while, young Blades, just for a few hours? I'll wake Kyla soon to take a second watch, and I can take third before your turn comes around. Sound reasonable?"

"Sounds fine to me," Brenna sighed, already unwinding on the grass next to Jess. Shann spread the blanket to cover her as well, and Brenna grinned when she felt her tuck it securely beneath her side. "Does anyone in Tristaine ever accuse you of mothering them, Shann?"

"Frequently, and I'm honored by it. Our word for 'mother' is a prayer, too." Shann bent and kissed Brenna's cheek. "Now sleep, Brenna. That's a royal command."

❖

She ran in the midst of a herd of wild horses, surrounded by flying manes and large, liquid eyes rolling in stark terror. Then she felt, more than heard, the timpani of drumming hooves in panicked flight all around her.

Brenna and her stallion plunged headlong through the forest with the rest of the herd, and the acrid smell of the smoke finally reached her, as fire began to ravage the woods around them—

"Brenna."

She came awake with a shuddering gasp, darting up on one elbow so fast she almost smacked Shann with her head. She felt Shann's steadying hand on her arm, and she spoke as soon as she could breathe evenly. "Sorry! Sorry. What?"

"Everyone's safe." Shann's voice was low and soothing. "It's all right. Give yourself time to wake up."

For an unsettling moment, Brenna craved a drink desperately, but the urge faded. Nothing like a heightened adrenaline surge to start the day. "Jess?"

"She's better."

Brenna put her hand out and felt a moment of panic, in spite of Shann's words, to find the pallet beside her empty. She looked up at Shann, blinking.

"Her fever broke early in Kyla's watch." Shann was outlined in faint blue light, so sunrise must be close. "She's had a solid six hours of sleep. That's enough, until we get some breakfast down her at least."

Shann helped her sit up. Brenna raked her fingers through her hair and craned to see Camryn's face, half-covered by Kyla's curling red tresses, on the air pallet nearby.

"Cam's fine too, I've checked her." Shann paused. "Adanin, Jess felt strong enough to stretch her legs a little, and I thought that was all right. But I'd rather she not be alone long."

Brenna was already getting up, trying not to groan after another night on the damp ground. "Can you point?"

Shann nodded toward the dry riverbed. "She promised not to go far, so I expect the two of you back by lunch."

Brenna offered a weak smile as she tied her sneakers. "Did you bring some of Tristaine's coffee?"

"Of course." Shann nodded. "It's mother's milk to Jess. Go tell her."

Brenna nodded and limped toward the riverbed, still trembling a little from her abrupt awakening.

"Brenna?" Shann looked after her, folding the army blanket neatly. "What's this about horses, and a fire?"

Brenna groaned. "I still talk in my sleep, don't I? Sam used to tease me about it." She sighed. "Just a dream, Shann. I've had it for weeks. Well, first it was just me and this horse, running from something. Then it was my horse fighting another horse. This time it was me and my horse, and many other horses, and a forest fire…" She ran out of steam and waved vaguely at Shann. "Never mind me. I'm still asleep. I'm talking out of my head. Be back soon."

Brenna didn't feel Shann's suddenly intent gaze on her as she made her way down the rise of the riverbank.

Shann felt a warm arm slide around her waist, and Kyla rested her head on her shoulder, yawning.

"Everything okay?"

"Good morning, little sister. Yes, we're doing well. Jess is stronger." Shann put her arm around Kyla, still looking after Brenna with a bemused expression. "I'm about to cook breakfast. Want to help?"

"Sure." Kyla eyed her queen curiously, then followed her fixed gaze. "What, lady? Is something up with Brenna?"

"Possibly," Shann murmured. "I'm beginning to think we might have a seer among us at last." She pressed Kyla's shoulders. "Now, adanin, while we brew coffee, a few thoughts about the joyous, sacred, and profoundly serious bond of marriage…"

❖

True to her word, Jess hadn't gone far. She'd found a wide ledge to rest on, topping a bluff just yards west of the riverbed.

Brenna first saw Jess's squared shoulders and erect posture, as she sat on an army blanket spread on the grass. She was looking out over a dizzying vista of treetops below her.

After months of confinement, Jess was enjoying the view. Her eyes swept the green expanses slowly, with restful pleasure. "Morning, Bren."

"Yeah," Brenna replied pleasantly. "How about you move, maybe six feet back from that ledge?"

Jess turned her head stiffly and regarded Brenna, who waited on the patch of grass between the riverbed and the bluff. She smiled and lifted herself on her heels and hands to inch painfully off the blanket and away from the ledge.

"Sorry." Brenna winced and folded her arms against the

early morning chill. "But you're still weak enough to pitch headfirst off that thing, and I hate heights enough to just let you drop."

Jess eased herself carefully onto the grass as Brenna knelt beside her. "Better?"

"Thanks." Brenna sat back on her heels and studied her face. "Well, your powers of recuperation continue to amaze me, Jesstin, but you still look like a train wreck. How many shades of bruise are you capable of?"

Jess smiled ruefully and allowed Brenna's cursory examination of her visible ills, touching her neck to gauge fever, taking her pulse, turning her head gently to check her pupils.

"You're cool enough, for now, and I don't think those ribs will trouble you too much if we keep you wrapped."

"How do you plan to escape through a mountain pass with a fear of heights, Brenna?"

"I didn't say I was afraid of heights. I said I hated them." Brenna frowned at the tender swelling beneath Jess's eye. "I just won't look down until we reach Tristaine."

Jess raised an eyebrow carefully.

Brenna hesitated, then brushed a faint line down the side of Jess's angular face, tracing the path of a recent tear. Jess's eyes shifted, but Brenna kept her hand lightly on her cheek. "Just nerves, Jesstin?"

Jess rested her face briefly in Brenna's palm. "Missing home."

"I know you do." Brenna gentled her voice. "It must be terrible for Cam and Kyla, too, to have to wait."

"Kyla was right last night." Jess lifted Brenna's hand from her face and cradled it in her own. "Tristaine's council will be divided without our voices. There are those in our village who still believe negotiating with the City is possible."

"How can they?" An image of the fighting stallions flashed through Brenna's mind, and she shook it off. "After everything that's happened, after Dyan, and Lauren—"

"They're a very small faction." Jess turned her troubled gaze to the valley below. "And our elders, the older women, are all solidly behind Shann. They'll keep the others in line. I know they will. Tristaine was dearly won, lass. We can't lose it now."

Jess skipped a pebble over a ledge yards away.

Brenna didn't hear it strike anything as it began its free fall.

They sat for a while in comfortable silence, the morning mountain breeze chilling them pleasantly.

"I've never had a community, a home like yours," Brenna said, finally. She felt the smooth swell of Jess's muscular arm, warm against her own.

"It's something I want to give you." Jess stroked the top of Brenna's bent head. "Someday I hope to make you my adonai, Brenna. My wife. I want to build you a cabin in our village, a home to grow old in together, safe among friends." Jess lowered her rich voice. "For now, if you'll let me, I'll be home to you, wherever we are."

Brenna shuddered with a familiar, delicious weakness that crept up her spine as Jess's warm breath touched her hair. "I've never had that either, that kind of love." Her eyes rose, and there was a note of pleading in them. "It scares me a little, Jess."

Jess's features softened, and she grinned down at Brenna and nudged her with her shoulder. "Well, I know what Shann would say. 'Jesstin has her quest now, young Blades, and you have yours. Jesstin must bring you home safe, and you must find the spine to love her in the manner she so richly deserves.'" Her brogue lengthened the word "richly," in a keen echo of Shann's musical voice. "'That's your job now, lass.'"

Brenna smiled. "Beats the hell out of my last gig, that's for sure."

Jess grinned and started unsnapping her shirt.

Brenna smiled again. "What are we doing?"

"Drills. We're going to give you a spine-strengthening session."

"I'm sorry?"

"I'm going to ravish you before breakfast."

"Oh, no, you're not."

Jess nodded and pulled her shirttails out of her pants.

"Jesstin." Brenna reached to feel Jess's forehead, but she ducked her touch deftly.

"Don't worry about me, lass. I'm fit enough to take on a wee mite like you."

"The last time I heard that," Brenna pointed out, "my staff laid you flat with one backswing."

"Oh, wench of little faith," Jess reproved, and reached for her.

Brenna straight-armed her back gently. "Jesstin, you're telling me you feel well enough to engage in sexual relations at this time?"

"Sweet Artemis, City girls love to talk."

"Just checking," Brenna said, and surged hard against Jess, who squeaked in surprise as Brenna's fingers wrapped in her wild hair and her head was pulled down for a heated kiss.

The two women sank to the rocky ground in full, unabashed lip-lock. Both of them cursed when they landed, Jess because the stony earth hurt her back, Brenna because Jess did, but they did so without ending the kiss. Their tongues entwined and they rolled.

Brenna's clothing was half off before she looked up and realized how close to the ledge they were. Glancing down she saw the army blanket tangled around her ankle, and she thrashed upright in Jess's arms instinctively. Not fighting her, just following a gut-level need to regain control and back away from danger.

"Wait," Jess breathed behind her. Her strong arms were wrapped around Brenna's waist, and she pulled Brenna upright against her so that her bare back pressed into Jess's open shirt.

Now they both kneeled in the grass, looking out over a carpeted expanse of green, silent space. Jess's arm was clamped beneath Brenna's exposed breasts, which bobbed against her tanned skin, the pink tips swollen and hard.

"I can't protect you from this kind of fear," Jess whispered, nodding at the dizzying drop beneath them. "And this kind of danger may always be part of your life with us." She wrapped her long fingers around Brenna's cool breast and squeezed. "But it will be a clean fear, not the hopelessness of the City. We'll be free, adanin." She began kneading both full globes, and her eyes clenched shut as a carnal heat streaked through her.

Brenna groaned with pleasure, in spite of her racing pulse. The edge of the bluff still felt terribly close, but her tension began to drain from her as Jess's palm rasped across her stiffening nipples.

"We'll be refugees at first, Brenna. Perhaps for a long time." Jess worked her free hand down beneath the waistband of Brenna's slacks. "Spread your knees, lass."

She skated over Brenna's soft mound, then moved lower to discover that her thighs were still clenched together.

Jess slapped Brenna's sensitive vulva, hard, and Brenna gasped and jerked her thighs apart, feeling the burning rasp of the grass against her kneecaps.

"But you're not alone anymore." The faint echo of a brogue touched Jess's voice again. "You have sisters now, other adanin. You have me, Bren." Her fingers swarmed down over Brenna's damp cleft, probing.

"Jesstin…" Brenna's hips bucked as Jess filled her snugly, then impaled her with a grinding twist. Jess began moving inside her with smooth, relentless strokes.

"I'm a warrior, Brenna," Jess murmured in her ear, "And I pledge my life to keeping you safe."

Brenna moaned as Jess flexed her knuckles gently, stretching her. The rough side of her narrowed hand scrubbed against Brenna's straining clitoris, sending needles of heat sparking along her shoulder blades.

"Tell me if you choose a life with us," Jess panted. "Answer me with your body."

Brenna whimpered helplessly, her head fell back against Jess's shoulder, and then she exploded in shuddering pleasure.

❖

After they'd calmed down, Jess wrapped the thin blanket around them both, and they watched the sun finish peaking over the eastern rise. Brenna sat in the grass in front of Jess, between her long legs, her back against her chest.

Brenna was dozing, and Jess smiled down at her, delighted at her soft snoring from her parted lips. She slept like a child in her arms.

"Hey." Jess squeezed her gently.

"Sorry. What? Hey."

"Nothing, darlin'. My butt's falling asleep, though."

Brenna awoke in stages, letting the cloud-studded sky fill her vision, as blue as her lover's eyes. "Good morning, Jesstin."

"Morning, adanin. Welcome to the day."

They sat for a moment longer, enjoying the view. After awhile, they helped each other up and made their way back up the riverbed, toward the faint, spicy aroma of fresh-brewed Tristainian coffee.

About the Author

Cate Culpepper is a 2005 Golden Crown Literary Award winner in the Sci-Fi/Fantasy category. She grew up in southern New Mexico, where she served as the state lesbian for several years. She moved to the Pacific Northwest almost twenty years ago, where she now resides with her faithful sidekick, Kirby, Warrior Westie. Cate supervises a transitional housing program for homeless young gay adults. She proudly cites *Xena: Warrior Princess* as a much-loved inspiration for the strong women portrayed in her original fiction.

Books Available From Bold Strokes Books

Whitewater Rendezvous by Kim Baldwin. Two women on a wilderness kayak adventure—Chaz Herrick, a laid-back outdoorswoman, and Megan Maxwell, a workaholic news executive—discover that true love may be nothing at all like they imagined. (1-933110-38-4)

Erotic Interludes 3: Lessons in Love ed. by Radclyffe and Stacia Seaman. Sign on for a class in love…the best lesbian erotica writers take us to "school." (1-933110-39-2)

Punk Like Me by JD Glass. Twenty-one year old Nina writes lyrics and plays guitar in the rock band, Adam's Rib, and she doesn't always play by the rules. And, oh yeah—she has a way with the girls. (1-933110-40-6)

Coffee Sonata by Gun Brooke. Four women whose lives unexpectedly intersect in a small town by the sea share one thing in common—they all have secrets. (1-933110-41-4)

The Clinic: Tristaine Book One by Cate Culpepper. Brenna, a prison medic, finds herself deeply conflicted by her growing feelings for her patient, Jesstin, a wild and rebellious warrior reputed to be descended from ancient Amazons. (1-933110-42-2)

Forever Found by JLee Meyer. Can time, tragedy, and shattered trust destroy a love that seemed destined? When chance reunites two childhood friends separated by tragedy, the past resurfaces to determine the shape of their future. (1-933110-37-6)

Sword of the Guardian by Merry Shannon. Princess Shasta's bold new bodyguard has a secret that could change both of their lives. He is actually a she. A passionate romance filled with courtly intrigue, chivalry, and devotion. (1-933110-36-8)

Wild Abandon by Ronica Black. From their first tumultuous meeting, Dr. Chandler Brogan and Officer Sarah Monroe are drawn together by their common obsessions—sex, speed, and danger. (1-933110-35-X)

Turn Back Time by Radclyffe. Pearce Rifkin and Wynter Thompson have nothing in common but a shared passion for surgery. They clash at every opportunity, especially when matters of the heart are suddenly at stake. (1-933110-34-1)

Chance by Grace Lennox. At twenty-six, Chance Delaney decides her life isn't working so she swaps it for a different one. What follows is the sexy, funny, touching story of two women who, in finding themselves, also find one another. (1-933110-31-7)

The Exile and the Sorcerer by Jane Fletcher. First in the Lyremouth Chronicles. Tevi, wounded and adrift, arrives in the courtyard of a shy young sorcerer. Together they face monsters, magic, and the challenge of loving despite their differences. (1-933110-32-5)

A Matter of Trust by Radclyffe. JT Sloan is a cybersleuth who doesn't like attachments. Michael Lassiter is leaving her husband, and she needs Sloan's expertise to safeguard her company. It should just be business—but it turns into much more. (1-933110-33-3)

Sweet Creek by Lee Lynch. A celebration of the enduring nature of love, friendship, and community in the quirky, heart-warming lesbian community of Waterfall Falls. (1-933110-29-5)

The Devil Inside by Ali Vali. Derby Cain Casey, head of a New Orleans crime organization, runs the family business with guts and grit, and no one crosses her. No one, that is, until Emma Verde claims her heart and turns her world upside down. (1-933110-30-9)

Grave Silence by Rose Beecham. Detective Jude Devine's investigation of a series of ritual murders is complicated by her torrid affair with the golden girl of Southwestern forensic pathology, Dr. Mercy Westmoreland. (1-933110-25-2)

Honor Reclaimed by Radclyffe. In the aftermath of 9/11, Secret Service Agent Cameron Roberts and Blair Powell close ranks with a trusted few to find the would-be assassins who nearly claimed Blair's life. (1-933110-18-X)

Honor Bound by Radclyffe. Secret Service Agent Cameron Roberts and Blair Powell face political intrigue, a clandestine threat to Blair's safety, and the seemingly irreconcilable personal differences that force them ever farther apart. (1-933110-20-1)

Protector of the Realm: Supreme Constellations Book One by Gun Brooke. A space adventure filled with suspense and a daring intergalactic romance featuring Commodore Rae Jacelon and a stunning, but decidedly lethal, Kellen O'Dal. (1-933110-26-0)

Innocent Hearts by Radclyffe. In a wild and unforgiving land, two women learn about love, passion, and the wonders of the heart. (1-933110-21-X)

The Temple at Landfall by Jane Fletcher. An imprinter, one of Celaeno's most revered servants of the Goddess, is also a prisoner to the faith—until a Ranger frees her by claiming her heart. The Celaeno series. (1-933110-27-9)

Force of Nature by Kim Baldwin. From tornados to forest fires, the forces of nature conspire to bring Gable McCoy and Erin Richards close to danger, and closer to each other. (1-933110-23-6)

In Too Deep by Ronica Black. Undercover homicide cop Erin McKenzie tracks a femme fatale who just might be a real killer…with love and danger hot on her heels. (1-933110-17-1)

Course of Action by Gun Brooke. Actress Carolyn Black desperately wants the starring role in an upcoming film produced by Annelie Peterson. Just how far will she go for the dream part of a lifetime? (1-933110-22-8)

Rangers at Roadsend by Jane Fletcher. Sergeant Chip Coppelli has learned to spot trouble coming, and that is exactly what she sees in her new recruit, Katryn Nagata. The Celaeno series. (1-933110-28-7)

Justice Served by Radclyffe. Lieutenant Rebecca Frye and her lover, Dr. Catherine Rawlings, embark on a deadly game of hide-and-seek with an underworld kingpin who traffics in human souls. (1-933110-15-5)

Distant Shores, Silent Thunder by Radclyffe. Doctor Tory King—and the women who love her—is forced to examine the boundaries of love, friendship, and the ties that transcend time. (1-933110-08-2)

Hunter's Pursuit by Kim Baldwin. A raging blizzard, a mountain hideaway, and a killer-for-hire set a scene for disaster—or desire—when Katarzyna Demetrious rescues a beautiful stranger. (1-933110-09-0)

The Walls of Westernfort by Jane Fletcher. All Temple Guard Natasha Ionadis wants is to serve the Goddess—until she falls in love with one of the rebels she is sworn to destroy. The Celaeno series. (1-933110-24-4)

Change Of Pace: *Erotic Interludes* by Radclyffe. Twenty-five hot-wired encounters guaranteed to spark more than just your imagination. Erotica as you've always dreamed of it. (1-933110-07-4)

Honor Guards by Radclyffe. In a wild flight for their lives, the president's daughter and those who are sworn to protect her wage a desperate struggle for survival. (1-933110-01-5)

Fated Love by Radclyffe. Amidst the chaos and drama of a busy emergency room, two women must contend not only with the fragile nature of life, but also with the irresistible forces of fate. (1-933110-05-8)

Justice in the Shadows by Radclyffe. In a shadow world of secrets and lies, Detective Sergeant Rebecca Frye and her lover, Dr. Catherine Rawlings, join forces in the elusive search for justice. (1-933110-03-1)

shadowland by Radclyffe. In a world on the far edge of desire, two women are drawn together by power, passion, and dark pleasures. An erotic romance. (1-933110-11-2)

Love's Masquerade by Radclyffe. Plunged into the indistinguishable realms of fiction, fantasy, and hidden desires, Auden Frost is forced to question all she believes about the nature of love. (1-933110-14-7)

Love & Honor by Radclyffe. The president's daughter and her lover are faced with difficult choices as they battle a tangled web of Washington intrigue for...love and honor. (1-933110-10-4)

Beyond the Breakwater by Radclyffe. One Provincetown summer three women learn the true meaning of love, friendship, and family. (1-933110-06-6)

Tomorrow's Promise by Radclyffe. One timeless summer, two very different women discover the power of passion to heal and the promise of hope that only love can bestow. (1-933110-12-0)

Love's Tender Warriors by Radclyffe. Two women who have accepted loneliness as a way of life learn that love is worth fighting for and a battle they cannot afford to lose. (1-933110-02-3)

Love's Melody Lost by Radclyffe. A secretive artist with a haunted past and a young woman escaping a life that has proved to be a lie find their destinies entwined. (1-933110-00-7)

Safe Harbor by Radclyffe. A mysterious newcomer, a reclusive doctor, and a troubled gay teenager learn about love, friendship, and trust during one tumultuous summer in Provincetown. (1-933110-13-9)

Above All, Honor by Radclyffe. Secret Service Agent Cameron Roberts fights her desire for the one woman she can't have—Blair Powell, the daughter of the president of the United States. (1-933110-04-X)